ETERNAL LOVE

BY
DANIELLE WOLFE

*His love for her
goes beyond the grave.*

There is Hope

If you or a loved one is considering suicide , please call or text 988
https://988lifeline.org/

Eternal Love's Playlist

Burn-The Cure
The Thirst is Taking Over -Skillet
Bloodflowers- The Cure
Savior-Skillet
Collide-Skillet
Against the Law- Donbor
Lovesong-The Cure
Andromeda-Dance with the Dead
Prayers for Rain- The Cure
The Same Deep Water as You – The Cure
Disintegration-The Cure
Zero Gravity Dance- Fraunhofer Diffraction
This Twilight Garden- The Cure
Dredd Song- The Cure
Star Trails- Fraunhoffer Diffraction
Bruises-Love and Death

Dedication

To those dying to be alive. To those who long for eternal love. His love for you goes beyond the grave.

To my sweet Vera, you carried me through the fire.

His love for
her brought
him to the
depths of hell
to where she
laid at rest.

Prologue

BLOOD DRIBBLED FROM MY flesh onto the grass below. The flourishing garden we once had, now become a cemetery for the dead. Even my sweat turned to blood when my prayers reached heaven for her, searching. Her lifeless eyes caused the flame within my own to burn. My blood, the very life of God, spilled from my thorny crown onto her.

My love for her brought me here, to her grave, where she laid at eternal rest.

Prologue

Chapter One
Dead

DEATH IS WHAT I longed for more than anything. One less pulse of my heart. One less breath in my lungs. Like a small tease, death was right there... waiting for me.

Streams of blood formed across a porcelain white bathtub. It looked like a painting you would find in an edgy art gallery. Blood is the expression of my true feelings locked within. Wincing, I pushed the blade deeper into my skin. Death had to be euphoric. Who cared if it was premature or not?

Tears and water streaked down my face and back as the pulsing stream from the showerhead above me washed the blood away. I pushed the blade and inched the razor deep across my leg. A rush of adrenaline hit me with the pure comfort that cutting promised. The need to feel alive again could only be found in pain.

A pounding on the door stopped me, and my heart sank. I was no longer safe in the swirling oblivion I'd created in the shower. No, I was pulled back to reality. The pounding at the door continued. Crap! The razor fell from my shaking hand onto the bottom of the bathtub.

"I need to get ready for work, and you will be late for..." my dad paused. His voice was just as shaky as the night he found me here. He was concerned but also clueless.

I let the last bit of blood spill into the drain and picked up the razor blade—the very evidence of what I had just done. Blood spilled out from my wound. I panicked; he couldn't find the razor or see me like this.

Drops of blood began to hit the checkered tile floor. What could I tell him? My brows furrowed. I was starting my period?

"Dalia?" Dad called from the other side of the door.

"I'll be out soon!" I frantically blotted out the mess on the floor and wrapped the towel around my torso, holding it under my arms carefully to ensure it covered my leg.

He was hovering by the door with a towel in hand. Once I opened the door, eyes darted around my legs and arms. I knew he was checking to see if I was okay.

"I'm okay, Dad." I brushed past him and into my bedroom, holding my breath.

The razor, still clenched and tucked neatly beneath my towel, fell out as soon as my bedroom door closed. That was close. My heart pounded not only from the rush of cutting but from the fact that I was still hiding.

The fresh red wound on my thigh stung, but I enjoyed it. I tentatively blotted out the rest of the blood on my leg and looked up at the long mirror that hung on my bedroom wall. Reflecting my body messily draped with the black terry towel. I saw something less than what I wanted. Stringy black hair plastered over my shoulders and framed my face.

I felt betrayed by myself again, staring at my own green eyes. I was torn up inside, and my body even reflected it. This was why

I cut. The wounds inside only kept me from gazing longer than I had to.

I pulled my black tights over to conceal my cut leg. It would allow the most comfort to the open wound, as jeans would scratch it throughout the day. Plus, it went well with my black leather skirt and band tee—my current favorite. The skirt sat comfortably across my hips and added the curves I wished were there. I lined my eyes with black to match and finished by brushing out my hair.

With my hand still shaking in the aftermath of what I had just done, I opened the bedroom door to find my dad hovering behind it again. His trademark eyes of concern met my cold glare.

This was my reality now. After what I did just a month ago, he would never give me space.

"Are you sure you are ready for this?" he asked.

Did he see the razor blade or the blood in the shower? I wanted to believe that I had been careful enough not to leave any trace of what I had done.

"Of course, Dad." I let my voice reassure him.

"I'm fine."

My breath stopped as I thought over my answer. I knew that I wasn't ready for where I was going. I also know I don't want to stop.

Chapter Two
Unstable

"I BELIEVE THIS IS going to help you." he broke the silence that had lingered since we left home. Dad buckled up and watched me do the same.

The sunlight offered no mercy as it scorched my face. The warmth on my skin and the blinding light that shone through the window reminded me why I wished to die. Turning to face him, I found the morning light made his middle-aged profile and wrinkled skin more prominent. He turned the car wheel with ease as he stroked his scraggly mustache. He always did that when he was nervous. The brakes to his car squealed as we finally pulled up to a boxy manilla-colored building several minutes later, and his hand touted up the gear shift. "Call me if you need to, and I'll pick you up," he said without hesitation.

"Elise is picking me up at the end of the day." I reminded him, biting my lip.

He nodded back, gazing out the window as he took a breath. "Right. Don't let me regret that decision."

I nodded. "Goodbye, Dad. I'll be fine." The wound on my thigh brushed roughly against my leggings as I slipped out of the car. He was right. I might not be ready.

I walked up the cement steps and to the darkened glass doorway. Inside, it looked like a doctor's office. Plain white walls with abstract art hung above blue cushioned chairs and magazines spread out on a clear end table. A woman with brown glasses and a loose messy bun handling calls at the front desk darted her eyes toward me. She pointed at a clipboard for me to sign in. I clutched the pen and scanned over the pages, aware that signing this was basically a blood oath. My oath would be to the mental health system. A living hell is what it is.

I scrawled my name across the forms, "Dalia Madison," and sat on the chair closest to her station.

The secretary plopped the phone down and picked up the board. Her eyes skimmed over the paperwork, then lifted to meet mine. She forced a professional smile, coming to stand on the other side of the desk beside me. "Welcome to Sweetwater Center, Nadalia. Your doctor called in for you—"

"Dalia," I interrupted, and the lady's eyebrows raised. "I prefer to go by Dalia."

Her lips thinned, and she looked down at the paper.

"Well, I shouldn't keep you out here long then," she said, not acknowledging my correction. "Come with me."

She waved her hand and guided me down the hall. But it wasn't my legs carrying me, rather, an obligation to my dad. We walked down a hallway with soft brown walls. Everything around us was uniform, much like the hospital rehab. It was like they purposely made it look so monotonous. The receptionist pointed toward a room with a single gray placard indicating the word 'Nurse' upon it.

"Every morning, you are to check in at the nurse's office, and then you will go to your group therapy room." She opened the door, revealing a small office space. I stepped inside and scanned the room, finding it was much like the waiting room. Dull and painfully... medical.

"Have a seat." Another woman pointed to a chair beside a blood pressure machine, offering me a sweet smile as I approached.

My bookbag slunk down my arm as I plopped onto the cushion. The door closed to the office, indicating the receptionist's departure. The nurse eyed me up and down. I stared right back at her, narrowing my eyes.

A thick southern accent came out of her lips as she spoke, "My name is Willa." She peered at my black studded belt. "Tomorrow, don't wear a belt. Give it to me for now, and I'll give it back at the end of the day. Also, your phone."

She pulled out a box of phones and pointed at it. I begrudgingly unbuckled the belt and pulled it off, then handed over my phone. If that's the worst I have to give up, I think I'd be okay. I had to do a full-on strip search in the hospital admission.

Willa hastily grabbed my hand and pulled up my long-sleeve shirt. Yes, it wasn't common to wear a sweater In Louisiana, even in October, but I liked them. She closely examined my uncut arm with pursed lips.

"Your file says you're a cutter," she said slowly. "Have you cut yourself since leaving the hospital?"

"No." My chest tightened as I lied.

I turned and looked down at my boots. Nurse Willa put the pressure cuff onto my arm, checked my pulse, and scribbled something down in a file.

"Nadalia Madison." She paused as she looked at my paperwork, skimming over it.

"I prefer to go by Dalia," I added.

She looked up at me and then scratched out the name I had written on the form. "Dalia," she repeated. Her eyes flicked back up to me. "What really brings you in here today?"

"My dad."

Her gaze lowered down to my clothes again. She opened a manila folder next to the paper. "It says here you tried committing suicide before being admitted to the hospital."

I nodded. That night was my best attempt. The blades dug just deep enough into my wrist. But the silence of the shower lasted too long, making my dad wonder where I was. He called an ambulance as soon as he saw the blood pooling in the tub. Willa stared directly into my eyes. She had green, lifeless eyes like my own. Her skin wrinkled behind blue-rimmed glasses, the only thing that brightened up her worn face. A tense quiet lingered between us as I clenched the chair's arm.

Finally, she nodded. "I'm going to keep you on the same meds as your psychiatrist at the hospital. You've been stabilized enough to be released, and that's good. The goal of Sweetwater is to transition you to a normal daily life back at school."

She pulled out a piece of paper with columns jotted with different times and words.

"This is just a daily schedule for your reference." She set her arms on her desk and leaned forward as if she was peering into my soul. "Dalia, your recovery and ability to move on from here will be contingent on your ability to comply with the rules. Along with evidence that you have stabilized."

That last word she said was drawn long by her thick accent. *Stabilized.* What did that even mean? That I'd conformed and settled for less? Given into a mundane lifestyle? Gotten comfortable enough to grow old into a nice little career like her own? Now, that would be the death of me.

She beamed up at me from the desk. "Let me show you to your group therapy room now."

We walked down the brown hallway, past several rooms with the same gray placards. I couldn't figure out what they were or which way we were going yet. But I swallowed a bit in relief. She wasn't going to check my legs for cuts.

"This is the community room." She pointed as we walked by it. As I quickly glanced inside, I could only see a couple of kids quietly sitting at lined desks. I knew what the hospital rehab was like. Something was scheduled for every hour. Confinement to your room in the morning, breakfast, group therapy morning and afternoon, sit in the group room after dinner, and stare at the white walls till the end of the day. This wouldn't be so different.

"Here is your group therapy room. Mrs. Gracie should be inside already with the rest of your group." Nurse Willa opened the door to a hideous Pepto-Bismol-pink room filled with chairs formed in a circle and teens with curious eyes darting my way.

"Come on in!" Mrs. Gracie, who I assumed she was at least, said with an overly enthusiastic tone.

Curly brown and gray hair framed her heart-shaped face. Her smile alone was much more welcoming than the woman at the front desk and Nurse Willa entirely. Sincerity emanated from her face. She pointed to a plastic chair left in the back corner. Honestly? I looked around at the walls and the people inside them, holding back a frown.

Nurse Willa popped her head through the door after me. "This is Dalia."

Several other teens my age filled the seats. I focused my attention back on Mrs. Gracie in a chair to my right. A skinny girl with long blonde hair sat beside her. Her arms covered her chest, hugging herself as she slouched in the plastic chair.

"My name is Mrs. Gracie. I am the group and individual therapist."

An exaggerated sigh came out from the skinny girl. I looked into Mrs. Gracie's brown eyes. They weren't as tired as Nurse

Willa's eyes. She extended her hand out to me, and I shook it in return.

"We are going to start with simple introductions. Why we are here and our goals for recovery. Kaylen." Mrs. Gracie turned to the skinny girl next to her.

"Since you are so enthusiastic this morning, maybe you can start?"

The girl turned to her, obviously annoyed.

"You know why I'm here. And you know why these other people are here." she snapped as she stood up and walked out of the room.

The door slammed behind her. The girl's voice could be heard in the background arguing with Nurse Willa. A slight shuffling with a couple of other male voices echoed. Everyone in the room sat silent for a second before the voices stopped.

"We all have to be participants in our own recovery," Mrs. Gracie chimed, still perky despite the outburst. "Claudia, you can start then."

A girl who looked about the same age as me, with neatly tied up hair and lip liner, started to talk.

My wound tingled, and I badly wanted to scratch the edges of it. Leaving it exposed to feel the abrasion of my leggings felt so relieving to me. My mouth tilted slightly upwards as my mind swirled with thoughts. So much had changed. I never expected I would be here. The first time I cut was just an experiment with some nail clippers. The rush flooded through my body as the ability to control my own pain became my drug. As a novice then, I put my cut in an incredibly obvious spot. The outside part of my upper arm.

It was summertime, and eventually, I caved to the humid Louisiana air. There was no way I could keep wearing my long-sleeved shirts anymore. I sat on my front porch, sipping on my lemonade and reading a book, when my mother caught sight of the clippings off my skin. The whole week afterward, she hounded me about it. As my parents' arguments grew, so too did my addiction. Then, one day, Mom just left. Two years later, here I am in a pink group therapy room. Pain was the only way I knew how to cope, and it led me here.

"Dalia, it's your turn now," Mrs. Gracie's voice brought my attention back to her. "Are you okay?" she asked, her brows furrowed.

"Yes." I pulled myself from my thoughts, shifting uncomfortably in my seat.

"Can you tell us why you are here?" Her tender voice coaxed me into submission.

"I'm a cutter." I looked down at the pink-tiled floor, unable to keep eye contact with anyone in the room. How was I supposed to open up to a room full of complete strangers?

I clenched my hands and set them on my lap. The only noise I could hear was my heart pounding and Mrs. Gracie's pen scribbling along her notepad. She nodded along and etched with the silence of the therapy circle. The stillness of those around me made me want to scream until I woke up from this nightmare. But I knew it couldn't be that simple.

"I... also tried to kill myself," I said, putting an end to the silence. But that didn't make things any less awkward.

"It's okay. You can open up to us here." Mrs. Gracie smiled reassuringly.

An annoying beeping sound wretched its way through my ears.

She perked up. "Alright then. It's time to go to the community room."

All the girls stood up, and the plastic chairs made that awful noise when scraped across the floor. But as they funneled out the room I looked up to a guy standing by the door. Broad shoulders covered by a thin black t-shirt accentuated a narrow waist and dark-wash skinny jeans. He wore large combat boots with black buckles.

A pointed chin ended the symmetry of his face with high cheekbones. One side of his scalp was buzzed and edged while the other side held long black disheveled hair that swept over his forehead and flowed past his shoulders. His lean frame complemented his face as he grinned at me.

I lingered for a moment before escaping the awkward moment and looked back, biting my lip. The door had shut, and he was gone. Who the hell was that guy?

My hands trembled as I looked down at the paper.

"Where do I go next?" I asked myself. The tingling in my leg grew stronger. I rubbed the sides of the wound again. This was the price I had to pay for cutting an area of my body that I had to cover.

I walked down the empty hallway and to the community room with the girls in my group therapy. They didn't even give me a second glance.

At least in this place, I wasn't a freak. I was just mentally unstable like everyone else. Taking a seat, I pulled out my book from my bag. Silence filled the room to the point where it made me uncomfortable. Why did no one talk here? Was it some unspoken rule?

"Dalia?" Mrs. Gracie's head popped through the open door. "Come join me in my office." I followed her until we reached a door displaying her name on a placard.

Mrs. Gracie pulled out a pen and a file as I sat in the brown, overly plush chair across from her desk. Everything was so minimalistic in here, with nothing out of place. I guess they didn't like to decorate much around here? Or they had to keep things that could become suicide tools or weapons away from the patients. I couldn't even wear my shoelaces at the inpatient hospital rehab. Her office was as simple as the rest of the facility. The only difference was a couple of pictures strewn across the desk. Her with a golden lab and, I'm assuming, her husband.

"So, Dalia, what are your goals before you leave the treatment program? I want to know what you're thinking." Her bright smile reflected back at me.

"I want to..."

What do I want? I don't want to stop cutting. It was the only thing that made me feel alive. Blood was the only way I found satisfaction. This habit, though dangerous left me with a purpose—a feeling when I felt so numb.

"Learn new coping mechanisms," I finally said, forcing a smile. I knew what to say to get discharged. By now, I knew what they wanted to hear. They couldn't make me go to therapy forever, so I'd hide until they let me pass on through.

"Okay then." Mrs. Gracie sighed and closed the folder. Her eyes told me she saw through my carefully crafted facade. Maybe I was like one of the thousands of girls who came here, or maybe her job meant something to her. All I knew was I wasn't ready for any help.

Chapter Three

Lafayette

I PACED IN FRONT of the gray cement steps and black-tinted door that I met at the beginning of my day. *Come on, Elise. Where are you?* One by one, each of those in my group stepped out of the building and was picked up by someone. The black-tinted door swung open. A tall figure holding a black bag walked out, and I squinted in the bright afternoon sun. Was that the guy I ran into earlier? A black hoodie obscured his face from the light. The sun made him look refined. His pale complexion revealed in the sun as he walked down the steps, around the side of the building, and disappeared. Flushing, I glanced back down at my iWatch until he walked away.

Gosh Elise. No returned texts, just the time. I dared to look back up after a second. A barely functioning green Volkswagen sputtered up to the curb. Elise jumped out, holding up a set of jangling keys like she had just won a Nobel prize.

"Sorry, I'm late. But I'm here now!" Her face beamed with excitement. I turned to see her oval face, pale with bright blue eyes. Her roughly textured hair wisped lightly around her face. The sides of her mouth crinkled as she halfway smiled. In contrast to my typically dark moods, she was the regular optimist. Even more so today since I'm no longer confined to the hospital.

"Our chariot awaits!" She rushed toward the bright green Volkswagen she inherited from her parents. It had a nice dent in the passenger door and nearly bald tires, but Elise was elated.

"At least I get to be with you every day after rehab." I winked at her and placed myself into the car along with my bookbag.

She threw her bag onto a pile of magazines, surrounded by empty kombucha bottles and other miscellaneous items in the backseat. "I'm just so glad you're out of that hellhole." Her smile was genuine. "So, how was your first day?"

I shrugged, making a face. "It was okay."

Elise's only response was to wrap her arms around me. My soul radiated as her frail arms made their way around my body. Her warmth gave me hope that I could make it through this day. Our friendship was the one thing I missed while I was in rehab. I missed *her*. It was her daily reminders that things could always get better that helped me get through. She was the light to my darkness. I didn't know what I would do without her. A tear leaked out and trailed down my cheek, and Elise swept it away.

"It's going to be okay. Do you want to go to the graveyard?" she asked softly.

I nodded. She fumbled with her keys on her tie-dyed lanyard. The ignition turned a couple of times before it caught on, and we sputtered onto our destination. She always knew what cheered me up. The silence of the graveyard helped me decompress from my day, and I was closest to the people I wanted to be like. Dead.

To me, this was just like the classes that lined the halls or the cubicles that filled the corporate towers. It was just another phase of life. A place to see those who made it to the end of their miserable existence. We entered by the large iron cemetery gate that had a small chip on the side that I could push my hand through even if the gate was locked. We didn't have to struggle this time because the gate was already open. Rows of gray and moss-covered tombstones lined the cement sidewalks. Elegantly carved names with dates were etched into each. The dire gray hues that covered the graveyard were beautiful to me. Trees lined the sides of the tombs, providing shady places for rest. I stood for a minute to breathe in the cemetery air. Inhale, hold, exhale.

Simple things like this were a luxury after being confined to the stark white rehab walls. Early October was my favorite time of the year to visit especially. The southern air was humid but with a little taste of the crisp fall air coming in.

"I'm just going to borrow this." I spoke to a grave before me as if the body of the one lying in it could reply as I picked up a rose from it. Of course, there was nothing but silence.

Elise glared at me. She may have more respect for the dead than I did. I longed to be among the undead. To live forever, past death. The only alternative I found possible to this life was to be like Anne Rice's Lestat. His grave gave me comfort. Inside my inner being, I knew there was something more than this life. I stood before Lestat's pearl-colored tomb surrounded by a white fence. Like the little white fences, people put around their perfect suburban homes. The only difference before me was in the homes, they dealt with the struggle of life. The person surrounded by this fence no longer knew that reality. That was a simple fact. Something that I missed just barely two months ago, with my failed attempt. Which so far was my best try at making it to the other side. My eyes wandered through the rows of countless graves, and I sighed.

"The thought of being dead seems so peaceful to me. People in the grave never worry or fear... They just *are*," I murmured.

Elise grabbed my hand with the rose in it. "You can find that here, too, Dalia."

I turned away from her. Her eyes were always filled with hope. I wished so much that I could see the bleakness of this world through the rainbow-colored glasses she wore. She pointed to a bouquet of roses leaning on the marble white headstone.

"There is always beauty in this world, despite what's surrounding it," she insisted. I lifted the rose I held in my hand, inhaling its sweet scent.

"I see things differently... This rose reminds me of how life is. Everything ends. Nothing ever stays the same. Nothing lasts forever."

Elise stayed silent and looked at the rose. The way I saw things had been different since my parents' divorce. At that time, my innocence died. For me, it was the final nail in the coffin. The only place I found solace since then was at this peaceful spot in Lafayette Cemetery, reading books and enjoying the quiet.

"What's that?!" Elise interrupted my thoughts with a gasp.

She pointed at a small grave nearby. I bent down to get a closer look. A needle with a long tube was on the ground. Stains of blood marked along the inside of the tube. I frowned, standing up straight again as I looked away in disgust.

She removed her hand from her mouth, and her face softened. "You know Halloween is coming up in just a couple weeks... Maybe it's a prop for some photoshoot or something?"

"It's probably some drug addict's way to get crack in their veins," I said flatly.

"Let's go home." I placed my arm around her. I had watched enough horror movies and read enough vampire novels to know that there were many possibilities with the evidence we found.

"You want to go home now?" Her eyebrows furrowed in concern.

"Yeah." I stared down at the small tube and needle.

I wanted to etch away the possibility that something would be wrong in the sanctuary that I loved so much. She looked deep

16

into me with her worried eyes that always convinced me to live another day.

"Will you be okay?" Elise asked quietly.

I knew that her thoughts were stuck on the fact of what another night alone meant for me. I had just gotten out of the hospital, and she had a right to be suspicious. I could only respond with the one lie I told often. The lie I told everyone and even myself at times.

"I'm fine."

Chapter Four
High

I WAS HERE AGAIN. This was the kind of trip you could never come down from. It was called monotony, and it would forever rule my life no matter how much I bitterly wished to escape it.

"How was your first day?" Dad asked as he picked up my dish from our wobbly wooden dining table.

I glared down at the small ripples in the wood. We never ate dinner together, let alone had a real conversation until my suicide attempt. Maybe he was trying to do better?

"Dalia? How was treatment today?" Dad's voice snapped me out of my thoughts.

He threw our paper plates into the trash, and the awkward silence grew between us as he washed his hands in the kitchen sink. The only thing I could think of was the cemetery and the needle with blood. But that wasn't exactly what I would want to talk to my dad my about.

"It was okay. I'm going to bed early tonight." I shrugged, walking away from the table.

"Alright then. I'm glad you had a good day. Goodnight, Dalia," he responded with a smile over his shoulder.

My eyes couldn't bear to turn and look at him as I left the room. I walked down the hall toward my room. I could imagine his eyes glaring at me, that facade of his falling away when he thought I wasn't looking. My heart pounded as I took one step, then another.

"It's not like you care about me. I'm just like Mom to you," I whispered into the void of the hallway.

I stared at the blue suitcase sitting by the bedroom door, thinking of Mom just as Dad slammed his bedroom door. I flinched; he was retiring for the night. Mom took the easy way out. I couldn't forgive the fact that she had left me here with Dad to fend for myself. Entering my room, I glanced down at the small jewelry box next to my bed and looked down at my arms. Both free of cuts. My eyes strayed to the ceiling, imagining it all. The blood leaking, how it would feel as I dug the blade into my flesh. The blade inside would give me so much relief with the stinging and then, of course, the *hit of adrenaline.* Like a peaceful wave washing over my skin.

The desire to cut only grew when I thought of nights like this. When my memories threatened to overtake me, clawing their way through my mind. The pain within me grew until it filled my beating heart and surged within my veins. I wanted to release it from within. Seeing the blood leaking out was like seeing what I was able to feel. I could let out the pain. I traced the end of the blade with my fingertip. My thoughts turned to Elise, and the blade clanged into the bottom of the jewelry box. She would hate seeing me carved up. I could resist at least this one night for her.

I sat back on my mattress with the blade tucked neatly inside the box. I could do this for her. I pushed myself, sweat trickling down my forehead and tears straining. "I can do this." I banged the jewelry box onto the cut on my leg, wincing from the pain and collapsing back onto my bed.

Chapter Five

Invitation

Waking up before the sun rises should be considered a crime. I pulled myself out of the warmth of my comforter, blinking my tired eyes to see the small jewelry box next to my pillowcase with the blade still inside. My phone buzzed beside it.

"I'm outside."

A sense of relief ran through me. I'd resisted the urge to cut. I made it through the night! The only thing that made me okay this morning was that I woke up to my arms with tender, uncut skin. It was the skin I fought for last night. It was *myself* I fought for. And I won.

Three texts and five calls from Elise illuminated the screen. Crap! I forgot to set my alarm. I pulled a black hoodie over the shirt I slept in and slipped on the jeans hanging on my vanity chair. Black waves fell down my back from the braid I had yesterday. I rubbed my face, still blotchy from sleep. This would have to do. It's not like I was trying to impress anyone. The sound of the Volkswagen honking outside pushed me to go faster down the hall and grab my bag.

"Dad! I'm leaving with Elise now!" I yelled toward his room and paused for a second with my backpack over my shoulder. Nothing but silence filled the house. We are back to normal, I guess.

Elise stood at the door waiting when I threw it open. "I'm here. Sorry, I'm late." She also had a tired look, with her hair in a ponytail and her eyes lacking their usual mascara.

I frowned. "I'm sorry if taking me is a hassle."

"Of course not. I'm here for you." She gave me a reassuring smile. I knew that mornings were hard for her, just as they were for myself. Even if my family wasn't here for me, I knew Elise always was.

We rode in the car to Sweetwater in silence. My stomach turned again this morning, rumbling beneath my hoodie. I should've eaten toast or something.

"I'll see you later." Elise chimed, and I was again left in front of the brown building.

I turned my eyes to scale up the whole building, biting my lip in thought. I could skip for the day, right? I played the whole scenario out in my head. I would read my books under the tree nearby all day and just meet Elise back here this afternoon. At the same time, I knew the consequences of that choice. My dad would be called and worried sick. It would bring me back to square one with him. He would hound me about it, and I'd be grounded again.

He would hover over me for weeks, breathing down my neck with no respite. I was simply destined to face another day at Sweetwater Center. A slight chill came across my neck, almost like a breath, and I shuddered. This time, I knew it wasn't Elise trying to surprise me. I turned around to meet two piercing black eyes. It's the same guy I noticed yesterday. His presence that much stronger as he spoke.

"Your name is... Dalia, right?"

My face was surprisingly close to his, and my whole body jolted back. Heat rushed to my cheeks. Why didn't I notice he was this close behind me?

"Yes. And how would you know that?" I replied stiffly. He wasn't in my group.

He shrugged. "I may have overheard a conversation between you and Gracie yesterday. I'm Kris." His hand extended down toward me. A handshake...? His palm's softness touched mine.

Dark brown eyes surrounded by black liner met mine. His eyebrow had a small silver stud piercing through it. I looked into them until embarrassment caused me to look away to the graveled ground. They were so deep and soulful—it was hard not to get captured in them. He was so tall, wearing a long black sweater, dark jeans, and the same combat boots I noticed yesterday. His tall stature hovered over me, making my heart pound harder.

"You're here for the same thing?" Kris pointed at his wrist.

I snatched my book bag from under my arm, unsure of how to answer him. I turned to the dark-tinted windows.

Finally, I settled for, "We'd better go inside." I half smiled, turning toward the entrance of the building.

His hand stopped me, sending a jolt through my body. I looked down at his grip on my elbow, narrowing my eyes.

"What the hell?" I tugged away, glaring at him.

He held his other hand up, displaying a black card he'd pulled out of his pocket. Even though he was being intrusive, I kind of liked it.

"An invitation." His jaw tilted, and his mouth curved up as he placed the card into my hand.

His lips, I noticed for the first time, were full with a light pink hue that contrasted nicely against his pale skin. His cheekbones were prominent, edging a long, angled face. His eyes softened as he smiled. I looked away as heat flooded my cheeks. This moment gave me what I really wanted: the opportunity to look at him more. I looked down at the card he gave me. It was worn with black and red letters. A black shadow in the form of a bat was printed in the background.

Kris murmured, "If you're free tonight, you might just find yourself in a place you can fit in." With that, he walked into the brown building. Just as foreboding as yesterday.

I looked down at the card and back up at him before I could say anything else. Silence. I couldn't reply with anything but silence. He was so confident. He just handed me the card and left. What if I didn't want to go? Or didn't like him? He seemed not to care. I stood speechless for a few moments before tucking the card into my hoodie. At least now there was a reason I could come here another day. Taking a deep breath, I opened the door and walked inside Sweetwater.

Chapter Six

Rules

THE WAITING ROOM WAS empty this time, so I headed straight for the nurse's office.

"Good morning, Dalia." Willa grabbed a manila file folder and motioned for me to sit in the chair next to the blue and white blood pressure machine. "I need to check."

I pulled up the sleeves of my hoodie to prove to her I had not cut. I was so glad I hadn't given in to the urge last night.

She offered me a smile. "Don't worry! I won't always need to do this." Willa lifted my arm to examine it. "Just in the beginning." Satisfied I looked clear, she turned and led me down the hall to the group therapy room.

The door opened up to the same ugly pink room as yesterday. There were more people this time. Mrs. Gracie's face beamed as I walked in again. Was she always like that? Elise and her must be kindred spirits. It was like seeing an older version of her when I looked at Mrs. Gracie. I kept my eyes on the ground as I plopped into a plastic chair in the corner, a little self-conscious about how I looked because I'd literally just rolled out of bed.

Peering up at Mrs. Gracie, I quickly scanned the room. Everyone was in here. Guys and girls. But my eyes couldn't miss the one person I had just run into. Why did he have to see me like this? I should have known with my luck that this would happen. I didn't even brush my teeth this morning!

Kris was sitting just across from me. He slouched in his chair with his long legs extending out. His hair shielded his face, his head turned toward Mrs. Gracie, looking at her as she pulled out her notebook from her bag. Group therapy felt as awkward as having brunch after a funeral. Even more so when you have no time to get ready in the morning, and you're sitting across from someone like Kris.

"We are doing a large group therapy today to go over the program rules and a quick introduction since we have several new patients." Mrs. Gracie smiled at those around her. "Rule number one: You have to own your recovery. Sam,"—she turned to a guy in sagging jeans and a blue hoodie with neatly buzzed hair—"can you tell us the second rule?"

He cleared his throat. "No phone use inside the treatment center," the boy replied gruffly. Well, that was obvious. Each person recited a rule as Mrs. Gracie called on them around the circle until she reached Kris.

"Kris. What is the last rule?"

He looked up at her, and then to my surprise, he looked at me. Tilting his head, it was almost like a smile played on his lips that he had to hold back.

"No contact between patients outside of the treatment center," he replied.

"Okay, that's good. Let's begin our introductions then. Kris, you can start," Mrs. Gracie chimed.

He sat up with confidence in his chair. "My name is Kris, and I'm hoping to find some new coping mechanisms." His gaze set on me, and I swallowed.

How much of that conversation between Mrs. Gracie and I did he overhear? I shook the thought from my head, realizing that I was staring back at him as much as he was at me. I directed my eyes back to Mrs. Gracie just to look back down at his tall black boots. Or maybe this guy just knew the rehab rhetoric like I did?

Everyone in the circle stated their names and whatever they probably knew would appease Mrs. Gracie. Each problem stated added another layer of tension until it was my turn to speak. I knotted my hoodie's sleeve into a ball in my clenched fist. Opening up to others like this was the worst part of going through any treatment program. Vulnerability was the death of any pride.

"My name is Dalia. I'm hoping to find some good habits in my life." I stared directly back at Kris.

Stuck in my body, my chest hardened with anxiety. His eyes caught mine again.

Mrs. Gracie interrupted, "I hope we can all find a place of understanding and hope here." Her words sliced the tension in the room, shaking me out of my thoughts.

The rest of the day was filled with learning about triggers, coping mechanisms, and other therapeutic jargon. Despite this, I couldn't separate myself from Kris. Our eyes crossed time and time again. Even when writing in my journal, I couldn't help but notice the couple of times we unintentionally studied each other. Each time, my anxiety rose. Why was the sense of meeting him so electrifying? Besides his good looks and mysterious demeanor, there was something that pulled me to him.

I was relieved when the fall air outside met my skin; the end of the day was here. I scrunched my sleeves halfway up my arms and examined them like Willa had this morning as I waited outside for Elise. My heart pounded with the thought of Kris coming up behind me, and I turned to look through the shaded doorway. I couldn't see inside despite how much I tried.

Did he leave before I did? I nervously bit my lip and looked back at the busy highway in front of the building. Even the way Kris looked set me on edge. The way he spoke was different. Eccentric and enticing.

Elise's green bug sputtered up as expected, and I jumped in. She smiled at me as she glanced down at my arms, noticing my raised sleeves and clear skin. A small but significant victory. She rolled down the windows to the car and pulled out onto the highway, keeping to the right lane as she always did, her blonde hair lightly blowing in the wind. She drove slowly, always careful.

Elise was my best friend, and we related in so many ways. She was also the exact opposite of me, even though we meshed so well. She wanted to put her feet in the grass and tan in the sunlight, whereas I wanted to sulk in a dark corner and write poetry. She wanted to dance in a light blue denim jacket and bell bottoms to Elton John. I teased my hair and lined my eyes while listening to The Cure.

She was a real hippie at heart, and I was a classic Lydia Deets, to put it at best. It was obvious we came from two vastly different worlds. But we were inseparable. Still, I wondered whether I could maybe meet someone like me. I felt the black card Kris gave me in my hoodie pocket. Pulling it out and examining it, I traced the edges with my chipped black fingernails.

"What is that?" Elise peeked through her circular John Lennon-shaped glasses over to the card.

"It's..." What should I tell her about it? "An invitation," I replied softly, keeping things honest between us. Her eyebrows raised as she glanced at me and then back at the road.

"An invitation to what?" Her voice perked up as much as her face did.

She knew very well that we both were rarely invited to anything. I studied the card again, suddenly stricken that I didn't know what I was holding either. What *was* this an invitation for? The deep red-hued color in the shape of a bat caught my eye.

"I'm... not sure." I reviewed the simple text on the card. The bold red letters contrasted with the black background. *The Batcave.* It read. I looked back up at Elise as she diligently watched the road. Kris's words reeled through my head like a movie scene. '*You may just find a place you will fit in...*' Would I be willing to take the risk?

"Could you take me?" I blurted out.

"Where is it?" Her question interrupted my thoughts.

"Someplace called, 'The Batcave.' There's an address. 742 Royal Street."

She scrunched her nose. "It sounds like a place downtown. You know I'm not good with driving down there." I could hear the hesitation in her voice.

I stared at her, willing her to give in. Finally, she shrugged.

"If you want to... but it's downtown." She glanced at the card, then back at the road. "At the Batcave? Are you sure this will be okay with your dad?"

"He doesn't have to know..," I chuckled. "Not like he would care anyway."

"Okay, but promise me you'll be safe." She side-eyed me as she gripped the wheel tighter.

Safe? I wasn't sure how I could promise her my safety when I was going to something like this. A meeting with a guy I met from rehab in downtown New Orleans at a place called 'The Batcave.'

My chest tightened. I could at least give her my word and try my best.

"Deal!" I beamed back at her.

Chapter Seven
The Batcave

EIGHT O'CLOCK DRAGGED ALONG, and I fumbled with my cell phone until I finally just threw it into my bat-wing backpack. My hair clung to my face and neck, and I combed it down to settle on one side. Tracing my lips with the darkest black color I owned, I contrasted them by covering my face with a translucent white powder.

A tight tank dress that stopped just a few inches above my knees left my black-and-white striped stockings peeping through the tops of my knee-high combat boots. I pulled the boot zippers up my calves, endless buckles adorning their sides, giving the illusion that I spent thirty minutes just putting my shoes on.

As I stood up straight, they added a couple inches of height to my petite five-foot-four frame. I cautiously stepped out of my room to peer around the hall.

"Dad, I'm going to Elise's for a couple of hours," I called out.

The TV hummed with the faint sound of a football game. No response. I walked over and stuck my head through his bedroom door. He was already passed out on the duvet inside his room, beer bottle in hand. Giving up, I headed outside where Elise was already waiting.

She eyeballed me as she stood up from the porch's step. "You look especially gothy today," she complimented as I locked the door behind me and we went to her car.

I sat down in the passenger seat of her beetle with a grin. "Why, thank you."

I slightly pulled down on my dress. This one took me out of my comfort zone completely. At least the stockings covered up the cuts on my thighs. I looked out of the car window as the suburban homes turned into skyscrapers, bars and venues.

The darkness in the sky contrasted with every blinding light and flashing sign. Even on a Tuesday night, the French Quarter was crammed. Drunk partygoers, tarot card readers, eccentric Voodoo shops, jazz artists, and crowds of tourists on paranormal tours bustled through the city streets. The nightlife was always happening in New Orleans.

Unfortunately, Elise was subjected to the honking cars swarming around her as she slowly followed every turn and command barked out by the GPS. She was barely keeping up with the flow of traffic. Elise cracked on the brakes as a crowd of drunk frat boys walked in front of us without a care in the world. We must have been going too slow for them to wait for us.

"I'm on the wrong street again," she stammered between clenched teeth. "Dalia, I don't think I can do this, "

My heart pounded as I spotted a large black building. "Oh, I think this is it!"

Elise looked out the window and bit her lip, clearly unsure.

"Don't worry!" I placed my hand on her shoulder. "I can do this by myself. Do you just want to head home?"

She squinted and looked past me toward the dark, looming building with the red neon sign. "I don't know, maybe I should wait for you ..."

31

"I'll be fine. I promise." My heart pounded harder as I consoled her with something I didn't even know myself. I flung open the passenger door and jumped out onto the urban streets.

"Wait!" Elise stopped me, and a car honked impatiently behind her. She winced. "Text me if you need a ride home... or anything."

"I'll be okay." I nodded and hurried over to the sidewalk.

She still looked nervous as she sped away. Pulling down my mini-dress, I looked around just to take in everything. Crowds of people flowed through the streets, laughing and chatting above the symphony of jazz. I was a teen girl, alone... in a short dress and a few blocks away from Bourbon Street at night. What could be safer? I should have brought my knife, or mace at least.

Red LED lights flashed above me, "*THE BATCAVE*." My chest became heavy, and my breath slowed. Maybe this wasn't the right decision for me to make? I barely knew the dude, yet here I was coming to meet him alone. I fidgeted with my batwing backpack as I questioned my choices. Directly under the flashing red words, a tall, industrial-sized metal door waited for me to open it.

Clenching my fist, I let go of any sense of caution and opened the door only to find a second doorway before me. Steel walls created a tunnel that led to a pair of black French doors. I walked forward, taking in the deepest breath my corset-cinched waist could handle. Fog leaked out of the edges of the doorway, beckoning me inside. I stepped forward. No going back now.

Pulling the large wrought iron handle on the door, I was met with a tall woman dressed like Elvira. Two older-looking men wearing all black strutted past her with lustful glares. She smiled unabashedly back in their direction until her eyes set on me.

"Well, well, well. What do we have here?" Elvira 2.0 placed her cigarette on a nearby ashtray, tilting her head toward me curiously.

I stepped back a bit. I should have known. I was too young to be in a place like this. How would I have gotten inside? Clearly, I didn't think this through. I put my hand on my bat-wing back-pack and clenched it close to my small, obviously teen body.

Elvira flicked up one long, pointed finger. "Wait."

Her long black nails flipped through the pages of a weathered book on the tall, cryptic-themed entrance table. My heart began to pound faster.

"Are you Dalia?" Her wide, mascara-lined eyes peered back up at me.

"Yes," I responded hesitantly.

She grinned. "Come on in, dear. Kris put you in on the list." She lifted the red rope that blocked me from entering the club. "Your host will be at the bar shortly."

She swung her head toward a faint corner of the clubroom. A newfound confidence clawed through me as I slipped past the infamous red rope that separated me from the club room. Kris made reservations for *us*. I could hardly believe it. Heart pound-ing, I stepped into the alternative world surrounding me. I found myself in a place I had always dreamed of. A large ballroom with cement walls painted black. Deep red lights lined the sides of the room, and smoke covered the dance floor. A heart-throbbing beat reverberated throughout the entire venue as clubgoers moved with it. Never in my life had I seen so many people like myself. They danced as if each vibration swayed them.

Some goth clubbers walked past me and stared at me like I was ready to be eaten alive. Crap! Right, I need to stop looking like I was lost and head for the bar. My eyes searched across the room until I spotted a black bar with neon red lights shining down. The lights above it illuminated various bottles for every toxic concoction the bartender crafted. Across from the bar were velvet red booths. I rushed to them as if they were a safe haven for me, and hell, maybe they were. I could wait for Kris there.

A warm hand on my shoulder stopped me from running to the booth. I turned toward the force pulling my shoulder back, imagining that I would be faced by the dark eyes I met earlier today, I turned with a smile that slowly faded. A tall man in a jet-black suit stood before me. Where was Kris? In his formal attire, the man looked different from the type of man to frequent this kind of club. I tentatively took a step back from him.

"Who are you?" I tried my best not to cringe, though I did on the inside. My grip on my backpack strap tightened. I scanned around the room, looking for Kris. Surely, this was a mistake.

"Come with me," the man replied to my question with an authoritative tone.

I stammered out, "I'm here for—"

"Kris?" the stranger interrupted me. "He's here. Follow me." He waved his hand toward the crowd of dancers.

I looked up at the tall man, questioning his integrity. What if he was lying? He let out an annoyed sigh, turned, and walked past the booths and toward the sea of dancers. He had no regard if I trusted him yet. He was just like Kris.

"Wait!" I jumped forward and picked up my pace to catch up with him. I trailed after the man, putting my fears behind me. I'd gotten this far, after all.

I pushed my way through the dancers and barely noticed that he paused at the other side of the dance floor, waiting for me. Enormous speakers next to the man boomed with VNV Nation playing heavily and rang through my ears. He stopped just beneath the DJ, in a kingdom of his own that stood towering above the clubgoers. I landed against the blackened wall. The man laughed as I tripped over my combat boots. His wrinkled hand pulled something on the wall next to me. A slit of light shone through as he opened what seemed to be a hidden door.

Politely, the man waited for me to enter with a smirk. I slowly entered the door. I wish I at least had my steel knife in my back-

34

pack if I needed it. A blood-red hallway lit by candelabras adjacent to each other was before me. Black doors lined the hallway all the way to the end.

The man placed his hand on mine, and I yanked away. The way his mouth curled in displeasure showed he was taken aback by my gesture. In the candlelight, I noticed his jet-black hair and blue eyes. Despite his slightly wrinkled face, he looked a little like Kris. Maybe he could be related to him?

Every step forward made a pounding sound echo on the floor, and my heart kept in sync. I remembered the safety I'd left at home... or even Elise's green Volkswagen. The hair on my arms raised, and a chill ran through my body, reminding me I should know better. Why did I come here tonight? The words replayed in my head. *Maybe you can find a place you will fit in?*

The man directed with his eyes toward the black door at the end of the hallway, leading me toward it. I noticed tiny dragons carved intricately on the wooden surface. The door creaked as he opened it before me, and I cautiously entered.

Pale, picturesque people sat on deep red sofas scattered across a shadowy room, chatting amongst themselves. Some of them held books, reading studiously. Some of them held wine glasses as they talked in groups. Yet I stood there, realizing I was back to where I normally was... out of place. No matter what those around me were doing here, they all carried a royal air about them.   Deep mahogany wooden columns lined the walls. The entire room smelled like sage. Blood-red booths similar to those in the bar sat across the back wall. Each booth was separated by a black velvet cloth draping down around them. At least I had something in common with the person who decorated around here.

My guide walked past me and led me to a far back corner of the room. I caught small glimpses from others around us as we passed. My body became tense as I cut through the stares that followed me. I directed my eyes to wherever the man was leading me, immediately feeling a sense of relief come over me once I saw him. Kris was sitting at a booth alone in the far corner of the room. His demeanor brightened once he looked up to see me, waiting for me to join him. I couldn't help but admire how handsome he was. His light smile drew me in even more than his natural sullen look. He was like a supernatural being that glowed as he sat in the darkened corner. I noticed a small candle with overflowing wax on it at the back of the booth. Next to it was a stack of books. As we drew near, I spotted Edgar Allan Poe among them. Maybe if I was lucky, he also liked Anne Rice.

"Dalia..." Kris began. The man who led me in nodded at Kris and walked away. He continued, "I'm so glad you came tonight."

I clung to the edge of the table, allowing myself to get comfortable as I squeezed in. My teeth clenched, I glanced around at every person that looked like they had stepped out of the vampire coven in the Underworld movie. Their eyes darting to look back at me every couple seconds. I could not tell if they wanted to greet me or eat me. Kris took a sip from a wine glass in his hand. The red liquid inside trailed back down from the rim as he placed it back onto the table. It was a thick consistency, not like your typical Bloody Mary.

My mind went back to the room surrounding me. Kris was silent while I looked around the room with wide eyes. I hesitated to speak first, but his kind stare remained constant.

"How did you find a place like this?" I prodded. At least, we would start with that.

He gestured toward the tall man by the door who'd escorted me in. "My uncle owns the club."

I pursed my lips, then smiled. "No wonder he seemed so important-looking." I bit my lip as my gaze took in the regal ambiance of the space around me. "This room is..." I struggled to find the exact word to say.

"Beautiful?" Kris suggested with a soft smile.

"This..." I stammered, trailing off in awe.

Kris lightly placed the crystal glass next to his stack of books. "Well, we can say it's the VIV room. Very Important Vampires."

I struggled to ask the next question, but Kris looked into my eyes as if he could read my mind. As if he was just waiting for me to ask him. A smirk played along his lips.

"Vampires?"

"Would you like a drink?" He pointed toward the wet bar.

I flushed. "I'm okay."

"Are you sure?" He raised a brow.

My mind was reeling, and I had to go ahead and ask him.

"What are you drinking? Aren't you a little young to be drinking alcohol?" My curiosity overruled all dignity at this point. I *had* to know what the thick red liquid in his glass was.

"This..." He raised the glass only to take another sip. The red liquid lightly smeared across his teeth. He looked at the glass with a sense of sobriety and answered with a dignified tone. "Is blood."

"Blood?" I smirked in disbelief. "*Really*?"

I had read my fair share of vampire novels. Well, maybe a lifetime's worth of them. But I had yet to drink blood. That was a bit too far, even for me.

"Yes. We mix it with a bit of wine." He took another casual sip, this time with a ministering glare. He didn't expect my reaction. "It gives it a special sweetness... that no one can recreate or compare."

He lightly dabbed the blood in the glass. Many thoughts flooded my mind. Could I have been led to a room full of vampires? Actual vampires? I peered across the dimly lit room. Not too far from our booth, a man held an antique book up to his face. He was far enough that I couldn't quite make out what he was reading. He also had a crystal glass with a deep red substance in his other hand. His brunette and gray receding hairline was just above a pair of circular glasses, and he had wrinkles around his lips and eyes. Dressed in black from head to toe. He looked more like a funeral director than a vampire.

I brought my attention back to Kris as he cleared his throat. His eyes had not left me for one second. I dared not to look into them too long. His eyes were like two gems above his prominent cheekbones. They drew me into him every time.

I peered back down at his glass. Why would he invite a complete stranger to the back room of a club where he drinks blood? It made no sense.

"Why did you invite me here?" I said quietly.

"I thought you would like a place like this. It's as simple as that," he replied calmly, taking another swig from his glass.

His demeanor was so relaxed and put together; I couldn't help but feel nervous in his presence. I honestly had never gotten the attention of someone as handsome as him.

"And... you're the prettiest girl I've seen at Sweetwater," he chimed in.

"Are you mocking me, or am I supposed to take that as a compliment?" Despite how attractive he was, I wasn't ready for some random dude to make comments on my appearance. But still, what could I say?

"I'm not joking." His eyes stilled onto mine. The sweat in my fists became cold as I released them. Maybe he wasn't kidding?

"Why are you in treatment?" I pushed for another answer from this mysterious guy.

"I like to cut at times, really deep too. And Its court mandated in order for my Uncle to keep me." He shrugged.

Kris still seemed so calm as he spoke. Opening up wasn't hard for him, and he had no shame about his self-harm. I tucked my legs under the booth further toward myself. *Keep him?* I wonder what happened to him to get to this state.

"I don't care what other people think about my habit. Do you want to know what's interesting?" he drawled.

I swallowed over the lump in my throat. "What?"

"That you came here tonight." Kris continued to look deeply into my eyes. It was as if he was glued to me already. When he didn't look away from me, I half-smiled.

"Are those your books?" I pointed down at the stack close to the candle.

"Yes, they are. Are you a fan?" he asked.

I picked up the first book on the stack. Anne Rice's Interview with the Vampire tucked under the candle. An old black leather-bound bible, partially dusty, was beneath it.

"She is my favorite author," I replied.

"Like I said, it's interesting we met. You seem to have similar tastes as I do."

"And this?" I pointed to the bible. "I'm not so sure we have the same tastes about this one."

His lips quirked. "Are you sure you wouldn't like something to drink?" he diverted me.

I took a second glance at Kris's elusive wine glass. The liquid seemed to pull me in this time as I eyed it. Maybe I could savor this moment and try to be the vampire I dreamed of, too? I could try drinking blood.

"Is everyone here drinking it?" I hesitantly pointed to his glass.

He nodded. "We all are." Kris pulled the leatherbound bible toward him. "I don't read this too much. It's mostly for decoration."

He flipped the dusty bible open. Deep red letters turned, and gold-trimmed pages crinkled between his grasp. I noticed a serpent ring on one of his fingers; his hands were large and cathartic. His size seemed to contrast me completely. I felt somewhat intimidated by his height and frame. With his ringed finger, he traced across one of the pages.

"Leviticus seventeen is one thing we live by. Life is in the blood." He grinned at me. "Would you like to try?"

Kris extended his hand with the glass in it. The thick crimson liquid swirled a moment as I reached for it. My mind began to swirl with questions. Putting the crystal to my lips, I took my first drink of blood. The liquid barely spilled into my mouth before I silently cringed. It wasn't at all what I'd expected. How could he enjoy this?

"What do you think?" Kris grinned at me as I set the glass down.

I hesitated and pursed my lips."Coppery..."

He laughed. "It's an acquired taste over time."

I brushed the back of my hand on my lips, trying to wipe any residue that could be left.

"What do we have here?" an unfamiliar voice behind me questioned. A man came and grabbed the glass from the table. Kris glared up at him. It wasn't his uncle or even the mid-forties funeral director guy.

The stranger's eyes slid back to me. "Some fresh meat, Kris?"

His broad, pointed shoulders and tall frame loomed over me as he stood beside the booth.

Suddenly, my calmness disappeared. My nerves hit again when a woman stepped in front of him. She was drastically shorter than him but carried herself more strongly.

"Valentin," she scolded him. "Stop picking on Kris." She extended an extravagantly jeweled hand toward me. "My name is Vivid, and please don't mind Valentin."

Valentin continued to stare down Kris with an intimidating glare. "I see you have her drinking blood already?"

Kris sighed. "Valentin, it's fine. She just had one sip."

"Come on, Valentin." Vivid pulled his hand to walk away from the booth. "We don't want to bother them."

I glanced up at Valentin, and his eyes locked onto mine. He was just standing there. He studied me like Kris did, but in a different way. Maybe I was 'fresh meat' to him?

"Goodbye, Valentin," Kris sneered toward him as he walked off.

"What's his problem?" I asked as soon as Valentin was across the room and not close enough to hear.

Kris rolled his eyes. "He's my obnoxious cousin." He took a large swig from his glass, finishing the rest of the liquid inside.

"The girl with him is his girlfriend, Vivid." He brushed his hand through his tousled hair. It fell perfectly back into place after he pulled the strands behind his shoulder. I stared at Kris, unsure of what to say.

"Valentin is a joke. Don't worry about him," he continued.

I simply nodded. "Not all families get along perfectly," I replied with a shrug. I stared into the candle's flame flickering between us, my thoughts darkening. I knew exactly what it was like to be tormented by family.

Kris motioned toward the door. "We should probably call it a night. Who knows what commotion Valentin is causing in the club room right now?"

I imagined that Valentin was the classic jock troublemaker, except gothic? Who knows?

"Do you need a ride home?" Kris suggested as he began to lead me out of the lavish room.

" Yes, I do." I looked around at the space one last time. Who knew if I would ever see such a beautiful place again? Probably only in my dreams. He touched my hand lightly as he led me to the car and opened the door.

The light across his car glided across the windshield as he zoomed through the suburban streets. I texted Elise and told her that Kris offered me a ride home, and she told me to follow up with her. Unfortunately, I figured out rather quickly that Kris was not the safest driver. I was so used to Elise's precautionary grandma driving. Seeing Kris race through the streets with no caution was a drastic change for me.

"Is this it?" he asked as he turned off the GPS on his phone and the Smiths blaring through the speakers faded.

"Yep," I replied nervously. Now he knew where I lived. Maybe I should have had Elise drive me home after all.

"I guess I'll see you at rehab. As strange as that is to say," he chuckled at me as I reached for the car door handle, and I smiled back. That was definitely not the strangest thing I experienced tonight, cue sarcasm.

"Where else would I be?" I stepped out of the car, and a chill went down my spine. Kris zoomed off into the night and left me with a million questions.

I had read a little online about vampire clans in New Orleans. The information was still vague. Reddit can only answer so much. Was it possible they weren't just a posh club posing as vampires? Each novel that lined the black bookshelf in my room couldn't give me answers to my questions. They only further fueled my fantasy of an urban vampire world. As I slumped down onto the black comforter on my bed, my phone vibrated.

"Are you okay? Make it home in one piece at least?" Elise texted. I could practically see her concerned face through my phone's screen.

I replied with an, *"I made it home okay, goodnight!"* and leaned onto my bed. My pillow positioned my head perfectly toward the bookshelf filled with hundreds of books. My eyes glanced across their spines sticking outwards.

Bloodlust one of the book titles read. Wait... An idea entered my mind. If Kris was an actual bloodthirsty immortal, could I lure him with what he wanted most? My blood.

Chapter Eight

Vampires at last

My plan left me with a sense of euphoria. Blood slithered from my skin as I pushed the blade across the top of my arm. I saw something that was worthless in my eyes. Today, at least my lifeblood could answer my most pressing question. Was Kris a vampire? If so, he wouldn't be able to resist the scent of my blood. Breathing in slowly and closing my eyes, I momentarily reveled in the buzzing pain across my upper arm.

I tucked the used blade into the bathroom trash, covered the wound with my tank top strap, and buried it over even more with a baggy band tee. The door to the bathroom creaked louder than before. Or maybe I was already paranoid about cutting while at rehab. I hurried past the nurse's office and to the chair in front of Kris in the community room. He was seated at a desk in the back of the community room, just as sullen and mysterious as he proved to be at the club last night. His only response to me was a smirk.

My heart pounded a little harder as I caught the gaze of his eyes for one more second. I felt a trickle of blood slide down my shoulder hidden by my oversized t-shirt. It was a fresh wound. If he was truly what he showed me last night, he wouldn't be able to resist the scent of my blood.

I glanced back at Kris, opening my mouth to say something...

"Dalia. There you are." Willa stood in the doorway, offering a smile.

My eyes shot straight at her as I stood up to remove any suspicion. I placed my bag over my shoulder with the cut. If I was lucky, maybe my shirt had blotted away any blood trickling down my tank top strap.

Like my arm, my mind only buzzed with one question. Was Kris a vampire? How could he not tell my arm was bleeding? If he *were* a bloodthirsty vampire, he would have pinned me against the wall to devour me whole. Instead, he was as still as a corpse. I couldn't get the phrase he said last night out of my head. Each word fell out of his lips with a smooth, rolling sensation.

"Life is in the blood."

In her office, Willa pointed to the corner with the blue chair, and I sat down. "Arms?" She pointed.

I moved my arms out, turning the inside of my forearms toward her. I just need to look as normal as possible, and I would be fine. Willa's eyes traced every inch of my arms. Then she did the unexpected: She lifted my shirt sleeve. I didn't flinch but turned to see what she saw as well. Blood slightly smeared from the edge of my tank top strap. I gazed up at her with a sense of shame.

"You're the one I have to watch," Willa sternly remarked. "Mrs. Gracie will check in with you at the end of the day."

She turned and jotted in her folder. My heart sunk into the blue leather chair as she closed my folder. *Check in?* With that, she waved me off.

"You're free to go," she stated.

I picked up my bag and walked down the hall past the community room. For a fleeting moment, I saw Kris. He was still sitting in the never-ending silence that remained in the community room. I narrowed my eyes as I passed him. Still unbothered by the scent of my blood.

Chapter Nine
Paintings on the wall

THE GROUP THERAPY HOUR dragged on with Mrs. Gracie talking. This time, I had no idea about what. My body slumped into the back of the plastic chair. I honestly didn't care about my recovery. I wasn't here for that today. The only thing that filled my mind this morning was the soreness of my arm and last night's escapades. My breath became shallow, and Mrs. Gracie's voice coaxed me like a lullaby.

A fringed piece of paper on the corner wall caught my eye. The paper was covered in black, and across the paper was a figure masqueraded in a shadow. This painting on the wall was different, though. Dark, in contrast to the normal color-filled paintings displayed around the center.

"Dalia." My gaze broke off the painting and back onto Mrs. Gracie as she called my name.

"Yes?" I sat up rigidly in my chair.

She frowned. "Are you okay?"

"Uh, yes. Yes, I am."

"Good, maybe later we can talk about some things," she replied with a thoughtful nod. My fist tightened as I leaned forward in my chair.

"You can all go to lunch." She closed the group.

I stood up, and instead of waiting for the rest of the people to leave the room, I walked over to the corner with the painting. Black clouds with fragile white paint swoops revealed a young girl's figure. Above her was an ominous figure with dark red paint. He embraced her as a lover. In contrast, the girl looked fragile and helpless in his arms. Two dark fangs protruded from his smile.

The letters "KV" etched on the side of the painting. Was this Kris's artwork? I stepped back a couple of steps to catch my breath in awe. It was beautiful. I was left with enough time to gather my books and my thoughts for the next class. If this painting were Kris's, this would only confirm why I had the question. Was Kris a vampire? I turned around and found myself across from Mrs. Gracie. Her soft brown eyes looked deep into mine as she spoke.

"Why did you cut yourself, Dalia?"

I turned my eyes away from hers and to the tile floor. What was I supposed to tell her? That I saw Kris at a club last night, and I think he might be a vampire? That would send me right back to inpatient treatment again. My sense of self hit the floor, and the numb, overwhelming fear of going back to the hospital mental ward melted over my body as silence lingered between us.

"It makes me feel alive," I replied to her. That was all I could sum it up to. The wrinkles on the corners of her face showed more prominently as she smiled at me.

"I can understand that. But there is so much more that can make you feel alive, even more than cutting can."

Her words sent an impaling fear within me. Then, it popped into my head like a sudden epiphany. This answer... I decided this answer would be more interesting this time.

"Life is within the blood."

Mrs. Gracie was silent as I turned back to look at the tile floor. Her smile had disappeared. "I'm here for you, and so is your dad. We are here to help," she promised me.

"Hmm." Sarcasm exuded from my lips. "Where was he when my mom needed help?"

"That's something we can definitely talk about." Her gaze switched from confused to concerned again.

"I don't think I want to. It won't change the reality that I feel alive when I cut."

Mrs. Gracie nodded and closed her group therapy folder. All the tension that mounted up within my body left as the folder closed. Sorrow painted on her lips as she said, "You know, Dalia, if you are not able to find the help you need here, you can go inpatient again."

48

Chapter Ten
Regret

Elise was munching on the bitter granola bars she loved so much when she pulled up to the treatment center. I plopped down in the worn gray seat next to her.

"How'd it go today?" she asked between bites.

I frowned at her. "I could go back to inpatient."

"Why?" Her face reflected the same concern as Mrs. Gracie's.

"If I don't follow the rules closely enough here." I turned and leaned my head onto the window.

"Hey." Elise placed her hand on my shoulder. "Well, how did it go last night?'

"Kris?" I interjected, raising my head to glance at her. "It was... interesting."

"So, his name is Kris? What type of interesting are you talking about?" She smirked.

I leaned into Elise with discretion. Careful to not let anyone overhear me even though we were in her car, I whispered, "I think they could be vampires."

She stared back at me in disbelief. "They? Who are *they*?" she pressed; I forgot that Elise didn't know anyone other than Kris.

"At the club, I met Kris and an entire group of people. Kris showed me a place I couldn't even imagine existed before—"

"Really?" Her eyes widened.

"They had a special room just for their little vampire club," I added.

She nodded, but her head tilted to the side. "That's strange. Why would you think they're vampires, though?'

"His uncle took me to a hidden back room inside the club. That's the *actual* Batcave." I proceeded with caution in every detail. "Elise, they were drinking blood mixed with wine."

She raised a brow. "That's weird, Dalia. I know you like vampire stuff, but don't you think that's taking it a bit too far?"

"I know, but at this point, I'm trying to figure out if they are actual vampires. The people in the group looked normal, but you never know..."

She gave me a hard look. Of all people, why would she doubt? She claimed that aliens and bigfoot were real. Vampires were not too far-fetched from that!

"Well, if anything is true, I know vampire movies cheer you up. Want to do a movie night?" Elise chimed as she held my hand.

"Of course." I nodded. It was nice getting back into the routine of movie nights, graveyard walks, and just hanging out with Elise. I could leave the thought of Kris behind, even for a little bit. I didn't want to tell Elise I cut my arm just to see if Kris would notice. She loathed my struggle with self-harm, even though she had all the empathy in the world for me.

I stared out the window of the car until we got home, just to escape my thoughts of Kris or the possibility of going back to inpatient treatment. No, I was fine right now. Everything was fine. We walked inside the doorway of my house. Everything was uniform and brown, like a 1970s vintage home. My dad even had a shag carpet in the living room. I pulled the key from my lanyard and placed it on the key ring. We walked down the hallway to my room.

Elise traced her hand across the black bookshelf lined with B-class monster movies and an array of vampire flicks under the TV hanging on the wall.

"What should it be tonight?" she questioned, tapping her finger lightly on the back of the DVD case. I poured out another guiltless handful of chocolates. As it melted in my palm, I replied to her question.

"Night of the Living Dead?"

In the other hand, I scrolled through my Instagram feed. Maybe I could find Kris there. I searched the Batcave's Instagram page hoping I would stumble across his.

Elise pulled out a random movie reluctantly. "How about we watch something else?" She skimmed her hands across the DVDs again.

I should search for something else like the nightclub scene in New Orleans. I looked up another club's Instagram page- at least something I could find locally. The page pulled up a gallery of pictures of clubgoers, goths, cyberpunks, and rave dancers. It looked like a place I definitely wanted to be. I scrolled through the endless number of pictures only to find nothing. Not even a trace about Kris. He intrigued me deeply, and I just hoped that I could see him again soon.

"Let's watch '*The Crow*'! We both love this one!" Elise chimed.

"It's a classic." I set my phone down.

The search for information about Kris would be endless. Still, nothing about him online? No Instagram, TikTok, not even an outdated Facebook profile? I took a small sip from my Monster drink in thought, and Elise glared at me.

"You know those are bad for you," she remarked flatly.

A faint knock on my bedroom door interrupted her lecture about chemicals in foods and the dangers of caffeine. The light from the hallway cracked through the doorway and into my dimly lit room as Dad peered inside.

"You girls don't watch too many movies tonight," he warned.

"Monsters don't sleep at night." I grinned back at him.

I took yet another swig of my Monster can and raised it up. I probably looked ridiculous as my black lipstick smudged and faded with each sip. He shook his head with a smile and shut the door. I reclined on my bed as Elise popped the DVD into my old-school Panasonic TV in the bedroom corner. The tragedy of Eric Draven and Shelly Webster unfolded with each scene. We both gazed at the television as if we hadn't seen this movie a million times before.

Still chomping on my candy, I paused for a second to think about Kris. What could he be doing right now? Who did he spend Friday nights with? With how amazing he looked; he was probably swooning a gothic model at the Batcave. The movie got to the scene where Eric rose from the grave. His hand pushed out slowly from the ground. He had resurrected to avenge his love. Even though tragedy and horror tried to separate them, death couldn't diminish his love for Shelly. Eric trudged the darkened alley streets led by the crow in search of his lover. Brandon Lee's physique reminded me of Kris. He was just as mysterious as he was.

Elise glanced up at me with furrowed brows. "Dalia, why are you smiling so big?"

Maybe it was unnatural for her to see me smile like that. Eric Draven enthralled me as he painted his face to mark his vengeance to the hallowed tunes of The Cure. The mask he wore made me think more about what I longed for most. Even more than Eric desired vengeance, I had an inner longing for something, too. Every scene with Eric brought my thoughts to one person. Kris. He was just as mysterious and handsome as Eric. The love that Eric and Shelly had lasted beyond death. I craved a love like that.

"Elise, do you think there is such a thing as true love?" I said dreamily, and Elise looked up at the TV screen with me.

"Or is it just in the movies? Or the books?' I pointed up to my bookshelf with the entire collection of vampire romance novels in it.

Elise sighed as her reply marked reality. "I would like to think there is."

Draven soulfully placed the rose bouquet on Shelly's grave. His love-filled eyes looked up at her in adoration as he laid upon his grave. They kissed as he gave his final breath, redeeming the tragedy, he could finally rest. If only I could find a love like that. Even death couldn't stop their love. Kris's eyes were just as soulful. Could I find this love with him?

I placed my hand on Elise's shoulder. She, too, was stuck staring at the screen, munching on her bag of organic popcorn.

"Elise, I've got it!" I exclaimed. The end credits rolled on the screen. I stood up immediately and started rummaging around in my closet before pulling out a black mini-dress.

"I need to go to the Batcave! Will you take me, Elise?" I asked excitedly.

Her hand paused from grabbing more popcorn. "Why?" was the only response from her.

I spun to face her. "It's the only way I can figure out if Kris is what I think he is."

"A *vampire*?' she retorted with bitter sarcasm.

"No, Elise. Last night, I felt so nervous," I sighed and sat down on the bed next to her. "But it also felt so *surreal*. I felt alive and like maybe I could find a place that I fit in."

My wildest dream was that a vampire prince would sweep me away. I didn't completely believe it could happen, but deep inside. I only hoped that maybe, just maybe, Kris, would be what I was looking for. Elise's deep blue eyes met mine as she placed her hand on my knee. Finally, she gave in.

"We can go."

Chapter Eleven

Sneak in

I STEPPED OUT TO the hallway in front of my dad's bedroom door dressed in my normal black-on-black garb. The background noise of his game show was the only noise I heard as I slipped through the house, save for the rain pitter-pattering on the roof.

He must have fallen asleep. I cracked his bedroom door open, seeing he was passed out in his brown recliner. I reached for the front door as Elise buckled up in her little green Volkswagen outside. If it wasn't for her, I wouldn't be able to go anywhere tonight.

"So, remind me again why you're doing this, Dalia?" Elise chimed in as I slumped into the car's beaten seat.

I shot my eyes at her. "I have to figure out more about Kris."

"Right and to figure out if they're vampires?"

"Maybe that too." I nodded.

She turned the ignition and drove through the rain-soaked streets. Maybe I was crazy, or perhaps mistaken. If they truly were a real vampire clan, maybe they had intentions of sucking my blood? Yet what if I could be part of the clan? I would never have to live the mundane suburban life that I had. Kris and I could be together forever, like Shelly and Eric Draven. Right?

Elise swerved on the dark highway overpass. I grabbed her arm.

"You okay?" I exclaimed, wincing at the torrential downpour outside the car.

She squinted, trying to peer through the rain. "Yeah. just trying to see." The old beaten wiper blades didn't aid in her driving at all. Hopefully, this would all be worth something.

I got myself prepared for...well, anything at this point. I fumbled around in my batty bat backpack.Switchblade, lighter, check. Crucifix,check. As we got closer, I recognized the same corner we saw the first night we drove to the Batcave. And maybe all this *was* silly. Still, I wanted to figure out more about Kris and the vampire clan. My experiment with giving off the scent of blood at rehab failed. Going to the Batcave, the source itself, was the only way I could find out more. Elise slowly inched up to the front of the black doorway leading to the inside. Her hand quivered as she placed it on my shoulder. Her eyes looking deep in mine. I know from the inside she was screaming for my safety.

"Remember, I'll text you when I'm done." I glanced at the green digital clock flashing above the car's old radio. It was only 9 p.m.

"Try to keep it under an hour or two, please," she whined.

"I will." I flung the door open, dodging the rain and racing towards the Batcave's entrance railing.

The same Elvira doorkeeper was there as before. Her smile was serene as if she recognized me amongst all the other clubgoers that passed by her every night.

"Oh, I remember you, Dalia, right?" she said smoothly. Even though she was dressed provocatively, she reminded me of the old lady at the library checkout desk, ready to charge you with an overdue book fine. Her hand held the red rope leading towards the underworld club before me. Suddenly, I noticed it wasn't just her jeering down at me. There was a familiar face next to her.

Kris's uncle. Crap!

"I need to go." All the blood left my face. My hand had nearly hit the door handle when a familiar voice interrupted me.

"Dalia?" Kris's voice rang through my ears, settling my unease.

Why was I so stupid? Of course, he would see me here. I sheepishly turned to smile back at him.

"I see you enjoyed our company and came back to see me." Kris stood there with a grin as he tucked his hands into the pockets of his faded black skinny jeans. A loose black sweater hung neatly over his broad muscular shoulders and arms. He looked so dignified.

I nervously laughed, "Maybe I came here because I enjoy the drinks?' I replied.

I didn't want to seem too desperate. Kris nodded towards Elvira 2.0, and she lifted the red rope. The club didn't have nearly as many goths or ghouls; maybe because it was a normal weeknight.

"Come this way," he beckoned.

"Um, okay," I stammered, and Kris led me down the blackened path across the dance floor to the secret hallway.

We walked down the red corridor as he led me to the same black door as before. He opened it wide and motioned for me to go in first, as always. As Kris opened the black door. I noticed this time there weren't any pale, picturesque people lounging on the couches. My brows furrowed.

"You can make yourself comfortable. I'll be right back."

Kris shut the door, offering me the chance to explore a little. Glancing around the room, I noticed things for the first time. The room smelled of incense and like deep musty air. Maybe for the sacrifices they performed? I placed my hand on one of the soft red cushioned tufts. They were all in the same places as before. I heard a faint voice in the hallway—I needed to investigate quick-ly.

My eyes darted across the room till I spotted a dark painting on the wall. I dropped my bat wing backpack. What could this be? From a distance, it looked like the painting in the group therapy room. I glanced at the bottom corner of the canvas, seeing the initials "KV" formed from the black and red hues. Here, a woman appeared bold instead of weak. A man was holding the hand of the woman who stood beside him. Her smile, created by small white brush strokes, had distinguished prominent fangs. She was a vampire, too.

Another voice, this time closer was in the hallway. Right below the canvas was a large wooden wine cellar. I peeped through the cracks, glancing at the bottles. Did they store the blood in here? It appeared to be what it was *supposed* to be in them. Wine? Hopefully. The jangle of the doorknob caused me to jolt as the door opened. I don't want him to think I was snooping around. Which I was.

Kris walked in and sat down comfortably at one booth. I fol-lowed him to sit at the booth. "So, what brings you here tonight?" he said smoothly.

"Well..." I paused and looked down at the black table separat-ing us. "I didn't think you would be here. And I wanted to figure out more about the club."

He laughed outright. "I live here, Dalia. "

"Live here?" I repeated, my eyes widening.

He brushed his hand through his long black hair, uncovering the side that was shaved and moving his hair to rest on his shoul-der.

I cleared my throat. "I'm sorry, I guess I don't understand. I didn't know people could live at a nightclub," I admitted.

The door to the room inched open. A woman dressed in a long black skirt with a corseted shirt that accentuated her narrow waist appeared. Her eyes were jade green, and her skin was perfectly white. She smiled politely at me. She was tall and regal. Who was she? His girlfriend? I paused and glanced towards Kris, questioning him with my eyes. I felt my heart pounding and my lips trembling. Maybe it was my insecurities. But I looked back up to find the woman now above me. She was much better looking than I was for sure.

"I left for a second because I wanted you to meet my mother." Instantly, relief flooded my body.

"Your mother?" I questioned, looking at the beautiful woman. She sat down next to Kris in the booth.

She looked at me with a light smile, yet in a serious tone she remarked, "I'm only ten years older than Kris."

I paused, but this time with confusion. Was this a joke?

"That's something we can talk about later, though," she continued as Kris laughed.

"This is Zayn. I can say she is *something* like my mother... Just like my uncle is like my father." Kris shrugged.

Zayn gleamed at me. "And you're the young lady I've heard all about." She eyed me as if she was adoring her son's little crush.

"You've heard about me?' I inquired, and Kris smiled.

"I'll clear up any confusion. My uncle and Zayn have been like a mom and dad to me since my parents died." He looked at me with a sincere twinkle in his eyes. Who knew what he had gone through and what it felt like to be an orphan? I could see that he was content with what he had. Perhaps that was a façade for him to get through life?

"I have found a family with my Uncle Alexander and Zayn." Kris looked at me again. This time without a flinch. As if he read my mind, or was I that easy to read?

"And we love having him." Zayn smiled knowingly back at him. "I have to get back to Alex." She gracefully left the room as Kris continued to talk.

"My uncle owns the club, and he takes care of me. I am normally here all hours of the night." Kris chuckled. "Well, I decided to live here too. This is my home. The clan has become my family."

I nodded my head to solidify what he was saying, yet I wanted to press him for more information. I pointed up toward a painting next to the booth.

"Are all these paintings yours?" I asked.

He nodded, his expression conveying pride. "Yes, they are."

I was captivated by the one next to the red booth painted with the same dark colors as the others. This one held shadowy figures encircling a fire.

"Do you want a drink?' Kris walked towards a small refrigerator next to the wine cellar, breaking my trance. "It's not blood this time."

It was as if he read my mind again, and he pulled out two energy drinks. I laughed nervously.

"So, you don't always drink blood?" I said, trying to keep my voice from wavering.

"Not always. Mostly with the clan." He nodded his head.

"The clan..." I paused. "What is the clan exactly?"

He looked at me for a second and his eyebrow lifted. I was prying this time. He placed his hand on the booth and stood uncomfortably close to me.

"The proper question is, why do you care?" He cracked open his energy drink can.

His reply left me silent a bit until I stammered. "I'd always hoped vampires were real. And I thought maybe—"

"Our group," he cut me off, "vampires? I'll ruin your fantasy. We are *not* vampires." He roughly placed his energy drink on the table.

For some reason, this topic angered him. Kris stalked back towards the wine cellar, and I peered after him. His hand brushed lightly across the top of it to stop next to a large candelabra before he continued.

"We may not be real vampires... but we come as close as we can in this life." He leaned close to me, his breath touching my face. Every piece of imperfection on his face met mine. Every movement he made was mesmerizing. Even the words he spoke.

"Dalia, I can tell you all about my life, my philosophies... my beliefs. But the truth lies within what you are seeking." He tilted his head, narrowing his eyes on mine. He was like no one I had ever met before. I was stunned by his answer.

"What do you mean by coming *close* to being vampires?" I said quietly.

"Come with me." He walked towards the black door.

We left the black room to go back into the red hallway again. I glanced down at my watch. 9:20 p.m. I didn't have much time left. I could hear the distant beat of the Cruxshadows from the dance floor. Across from the clan room's door was a navy blue door. This hallway was just way too much like a wicked Alice in Wonderland.

He opened the door and turned on a little blue light next to the door. Was he bringing me into a place that I would regret? I trembled slightly as I stumbled into the room, following behind him to a space that appeared to be an old basement. Cement walls, floors, and a small window close to the top of the ceiling. A pile of dark black clothes was piled in the corner. A large dark bookshelf was next to a mattress on the floor.

Kris splayed his hands, gesturing towards the space. "This is my room."

I laughed. I must have an overactive imagination like my mom always said. I walked to the black bookshelf next to a smooth TV screen mounted on the wall, similar to the one I had in my room. A myriad of vampire novels and horror movies lined it just like my own bookshelf back at home. I drew my attention to another side of the bedroom, holding an art easel with a collection of paints scattered across the floor. Kris stood next to me, looking with me at what appeared to be an unfinished painting.

"I'll finish this one soon," he commented as he walked past me to another darkened corner of the room, pulling roughly on a small silver chain hanging from the ceiling.

A red lamp above him swayed and illuminated every detail of the painting, revealing another piece of art with shadowy figures made with shades of dark green, blue, and black. I turned back toward the door when I realized I had missed what Kris was trying to show me. The red light slowly stopped its sway above a dark wooden coffin lying on the floor. I blinked to double check that I wasn't just imagining things. Kris eyed me. His gaze never moved from me. This was real.

"Do I sleep in there?" Kris stated in a joking tone as if he was trying to answer the question I may have been thinking. "No, I don't." He laid his hand on the coffin lid firmly. "But someday, I will."

"You're serious about this vampire stuff," I replied, my voice low.

"We are all going to die someday. Right, Dalia?"

I stood there in silence, staring at the old wooden coffin, taking in the implications of his words. He stepped toward the moonlight coming through the small window in the dark corner of the room.

He was kind of like the guy I had always imagined I would be with. Dark, elusive... vampiric. Even though he wasn't a real vampire.

"Right," I replied to him, swallowing anxiously.

The coffin had a small black rose bouquet laid upon it, and I tentatively placed my hand on it. As much as I wanted to interrogate him this time, I also wanted to show him instead that

I accepted him. I turned to the opposite side of the room and pointed to the unmade black mattress on the floor.

"*That's* where you sleep." I smiled at him, and Kris pointed to a small black futon he had across from the TV mounted on the wall.

"Have a seat." He gestured as he removed a pillow on it to give me room.

The bookshelf revealed all the horror flicks and gothic books I could imagine. "It seems you like a lot of the same movies and books I do."

Kris shrugged. "That's not a surprise to me." He sat on the other side of the futon.

"So, Dalia, why did you come here tonight?"

Heat flushed to my cheeks. "Simple. I wanted to know more about you..." I paused with a slight grin. " but I feel like the more I know about you, the more questions I have."

My phone buzzed, and my blood ran cold, ruining the moment. Crap! What time was it? I pulled out my watch. It was 9:58. Elise was calling.

I bit my lip, glancing up at Kris. "I have to go."

I stepped toward the door, but a sudden chill overwhelmed me when my hand hit the doorknob. Kris's hand on my shoulder caused me to stop. *His lovely hand.*

I turned around, seeing he had a glimmer in his eyes.

"Let me walk you out." He offered his hand. I couldn't deny the fact that a sense of electricity ran through me as my palm touched his. There was something different about him. We walked down the blood-red hallway, across the blackened dance floor, and to Elvira 2.0 at the entrance. It almost felt like a part of me was saying goodbye. I was closing another chapter in this mystery. Kris wasn't a vampire, but I found out more tonight. He was just as interested in me as I was in him. And maybe, just maybe, that discovery was even better.

I climbed back inside Elise's car, my shoes slick from the damp pavement. She smiled at me as Kris opened the door and walked away. The rain that was pouring hard earlier had now ceased. I felt like my emotions were just as unpredictable as the weather in New Orleans. I now had more questions than before I came. Why did he have a coffin in his room? What did he mean that he would sleep in it someday? Why didn't I just ask him about the coffin? How did his parents die? Maybe it was his eyes that pulled and dragged me into him. Maybe it was the sway of two introverted souls finally finding peace in a macabre connection. When I was with Kris, I wasn't haunted by the questions spinning in my head when I was away. A part of me just wanted to be with him. Elise glanced at me from the wheel of the car.

"I can assume it went well? They didn't drink your blood and leave you for dead." She smirked as she drove down the highway the same slow pace as usual.

"Well, they aren't vampires." I leaned my head against the car's window. The muggy heat from the rain had begun to fog up the glass. "But they *are* a vampire clan... and I'm still not sure what that means."

Elise looked over at me in a serious manner. "That might not be something you want to find out."

"He showed me his bedroom." I bit my lip, hesitantly looking at her.

Her eyebrows nearly shot up to her hairline. "And what happened?" she pressed eagerly.

I scoffed. "He just wanted to show me his room."

"Oh, really?" She winked at me.

"*And* he has a real coffin in his bedroom!"

Elise's face tilted back as she blew out a sigh. "Dalia, are you sure this guy isn't crazy?"

I placed my hand on hers. Her worrying would never stop if I didn't. "It's fine, I promise," I reassured her with my most convincing look.

Elise nodded in silence, and we continued driving back to my place. "I'll see you tomorrow after school at the treatment center." As I closed the door to her beetle. Closing the door to the adventure I had tonight.

Chapter Twelve
Death
Sentence

THE COMMUNITY ROOM DURING lunch had the same dingy heat that came in from outside. I slouched into a desk and grabbed my journal to take advantage of the only time of day I could write. A small sigh exited my lungs, and I clenched my pen. I continued with the words that came to my mind about everything that was holding me here.

"I long to be one with death. To have my soul entwined with it. To have my body wrapped up in it. The coffin, as my lair. The ground hollowing around me as I'm sinking into oblivion. The worms are my friends. The air above the grave is my song. It sings for nothing and no one. To be dead is to not exist. To not exist is my innermost longing. If I were to draw my last breath, I would want it to be with you. The one thing that is keeping me here is the promise of eternal love and life beyond the grave."

My pen dropped, and I clenched my teeth. A slight splatter of ink marked the words I had just written on the page. It hit me again. The reality that death was what I'd been longing for. Perhaps what I need is to find something that is worth dying for?

Last night, I got to see a whole new side of Kris. I learned more about his family, the clan, and that they weren't vampires. Despite what I had learned, I still felt the longing to learn more.

"The life of a creature is within the blood." Kris raised the glass to his lips.

The words swirled in my mind just as the blood and wine did in the chalice he drank from. The desire to die haunted me. It was like it called me as my destiny. This must be why I was also drawn to the clan. Had they found the answer to death and immortality?

Mrs. Gracie popped her head through the community room door. Her eyebrows lifted and her forehead wrinkled, a slight upward smile on her face.

"Dalia, can you come to my office for a minute?" My breath slowed down as I stood up. Why did I get called into her office the morning after I had spent time with Kris last night? Was this going to be some intervention or... an investigation? Would they tell me to never talk to him again?

I could feel my heart beating faster as I sat in the brown tuft chair across from Mrs. Gracie's desk. Immediately, her eyes met mine. I wouldn't let them get to me. I couldn't let them.

"So, Dalia. I brought you in here because I wanted to know your thoughts. What do you think triggered you to self-harm the other day?" Her question caught me off guard.

"What do you mean?" I deflected. Even this was something I didn't want to talk to her about, but her eyes refused to divert from mine.

"I mean why did you cut your shoulder the other day, Dalia?"

I attempted to keep my face neutral.

"Perhaps I enjoy it," I said briskly.

"Okay, Dalia." She closed the blue file folder in front of her with a sigh. "I want you to promise me that tonight at least you will try one of the coping mechanisms we talked about in group therapy this morning before acting out on any self-harm. Can we start with that?"

I could promise her nothing. But I wasn't going to say that.

"You can only do this for you. No one else," she added soulfully.

She reminded me so much of Elise. Maybe that was what I needed. Elise always knew how to lift my spirits. Despite the distance between her desk, I felt that I wanted to hug Mrs. Gracie. To melt in her arms and let her hair absorb my tears. That was the last memory I had of my mother. I was melting into her arms, smelling the soft waves of her hair underneath my nose as we both cried.

My mother's voice trembled as she said the same phrase over and over again in my ear. "I'm so sorry." Then she left.

I clenched the edges of the arms of my chair. The rough wood brought me back to where I was. Sitting across from Mrs. Gracie. Her worried eyes met mine again. I walked through the rest of my day feeling distant and numb to my surroundings. Elise became my salvation from my dissociation when she pulled up in the bright green Volkswagen.

"Speak of the devil himself," she said as I sat down in the passenger seat, throwing a couple of empty cans over into the back.

I turned around, peering through the rear window to see Kris clad in his perfect combat boots, tattered jeans, and a loose cotton black t-shirt. He ran his hand through his shoulder-length hair as he stepped out onto the steps I was just waiting on, his eyes catching mine.

"He's coming this way," I whispered to Elise, trying my best to not seem nervous as she just shook her head at me.

I got a good glimpse of just his chest in the window until he stooped down and smiled. My brain hit pause for a moment until I realized I had to roll down the window to hear him. I pulled the old lever, not automatic, to get the window cranked down.

"May I speak with you?" He had such a formal tone and a slight grin as he spoke this time.

Elise just continued to look at me. Even *she* was blushing. I sat with anticipation of what he would say.

"Can I pick you up at your place at seven?" His mouth formed the words, and time seemed to still for a moment. He wanted to come pick me up at my place? Dark eyes met mine as I stared back up into them.

I nodded silently, even though I was dying on the inside from a hurricane of butterflies. He didn't seem fazed by my silence.

"I wanted to show you something. It's a surprise. Are you cool with that?" he continued.

"As long as it isn't another coffin," I replied sarcastically. As if that remark helped hide the fact that my heart was beating a hundred beats per second.

"At least I won't have to drive her this time," Elise sheepishly jabbed in.

A light smile crossed Kris's face as his eyes moved towards Elise and then back at me. She always knew how to kill the perfect moment.

The real death sentence didn't meet me until after dinner when Dad had me wash dishes. I rinsed the dishes and plopped them into the dishwasher. I didn't want to have to do this before seeing Kris, but Dad insisted that I do a load of dishes *right now*.

Can you get any louder doing that?" Dad groaned as he finished eating his last slice of pizza.

I sighed and slowed down my pace just a little. "I want to go out and meet a friend."

"Why are you in such a hurry? You can invite Elise over if you want to," Dad added.

I scrubbed diligently at the last plate. The crust on it was relentless.

"Elise?" I chuckled, but I guess he had a good reason to think my only friend was Elise. Up until this week, he would have been right. He stood up from the dining table and shoved his plate in my direction. I smiled halfheartedly and grabbed the dish that had promptly ruined my hopes of dish duty being over.

He chimed in what I had also feared, "Try not to be out too late."

"Okay, Dad." I slammed the dishwasher door shut with relief before leaning against the kitchen counter.

Hopefully, I could get out of the house before he noticed what I was wearing again. Back in my room, I stretched my black stockings across my legs as I pulled them up to my blood-red skirt. A loose-knit sweater draped neatly over my waist, and I tied my black hair up into pigtails before adding a thick layer of dark red to my eyelids.

I clenched my bat wing backpack around my arm and opened the front door. A slick black Charger was parked in front of the house, its engine rumbling. I exhaled, releasing the tension for the night with my breath as I approached the car. Salvation! I made it out without my dad noticing who was picking me up. I slipped into the black leather passenger seat. Kris pushed a button in his rearview mirror and the sunroof opened above us.

I looked up at the cloudy night sky. It was beautiful. "I wish we could see the stars better here." I sighed.

He put his hand on the gear and turned on the growling ignition. Louder than it should have been.

"Where are we going?" I prodded him, raising a brow.

He smirked. "That is part of the surprise." I peeked up out of the sunroof again. Could this get any better? Even though I had only known Kris for a week, I couldn't help but feel connected to him.

We raced down several long winding roads while I imagined myself being whisked away into the night by a vampire prince. If I was afraid, I could lay my head on his chest. His arms would wash away any depression. Our nights together would last for eternity as we live in a vampiric bliss at the Batcave. I would be who I wanted to be. I fixed my eyes on the radio pulsating with the Smiths, then on Kris's hand resting on the wheel, and then to his perfect profile as he drove. Each streetlight illuminated his flawless skin and well-proportioned face. Whenever I looked at him, I fell into a deep pit of admiration.

A smile crossed his face once he noticed I was looking at him. Even though he was driving at a lethal speed; his speed alone showed his *real* value for life. I turned to stare out the window again and watched the suburban homes fly by. Every moment he drove was just another second I savored being with him. Yet the minutes soon turned into an hour, and the buildings outside eventually became unfamiliar to me. The suburbs faded into a deep forest as we drove past the city limits.

Chapter Thirteen
Fire Baptism

THE SCENT OF SMOKE filled my nostrils as I stared into the pitch-black forest. Trees barricaded us like a deep, thick wall. The surrounding darkness grew once he switched off the ignition and the headlights dimmed. My hand slipped as I tried to open the car door. As my eyes adjusted to the dark, fear grew within me. Louisiana's forests were never silent as the hum of cicadas and toads filled the air. A sound only the deep south could provide. Guiding myself out of the car, I reached for the Charger's front hood, finding it was still warm from the long drive.

"You okay?" Kris's voice close to my ear made me jump. He was next to me already, catching my hand as I stumbled.

'It's the boots." I laughed, even though I was more embarrassed than flattered that he'd prevented me from falling flat on my face.

"Where are you taking me?" I glanced at my watch —10:30 p.m.

"You'll see." He winked.

What kind of surprise was Kris taking me to? Why was there the scent of... I paused for a moment to breathe in. Something burning? What the hell had I gotten myself into? Did he bring me here to tie me up, fulfill his desires, and leave me for dead? In the distance, small flames dancing on top of a circle of totem poles caught my eye. Was this a ritual for the clan?

Kris guided me towards the flames, but I stopped in my tracks, causing him to jolt. My eyes looked up to confirm what I was thinking. Through the trees, the moon beamed its silver light.

"It's a crescent moon." Hesitation cracked in my voice. My panicked eyes met Kris's calm stare.

He delicately placed his hand on my shoulder. "This is an initiation between the members of our clan. Not everyone can come to these, but you're with me," he explained.

"I'm with you?" Fear echoed in my words.

His sturdy hand on my shoulder glided down my arm to take my hand securely in his. "So, you're good," he replied. "Do you trust me?"

Did I? His undeniable eyes persuaded me. I turned toward the circle again, with the faint voices of clan members gathering around the bonfire. Staying close to Kris, I moved with him as the clan members gathered toward the bonfire. Who was I to be here? Whatever they were doing, without a doubt, it intimidated me. If I took a chance, maybe I could find a place with them. Or not just with them, but with him. I turned to face Kris, biting my lip.

"Okay." I finally nodded. His grin matched the moonlight as he led me towards the gathering.

There appeared to be a smaller number of clan members compared to the first night at the Batcave. Zayn and Alex stood on the outer edge of the encircling members. Dressed in a leather trench coat, Alex's arms were crossed as if he were guarding the vicinity.

Zayn stood next to him, looking perfect, dressed in a deep red chiffon dress. Her jade green eyes were visible in the firelight. The countenance she had was that of royalty as she stared into the flames. I couldn't help but wonder what her life was like. She was like a queen of the night. Her life had to be full of adventure.

Kris led me closer to the encircling members. Pale faces with menacing glares slowly turned towards me. I wasn't welcome. I lowered my head as if I could hide. Kris promptly let go of my hand as I sat down on a large rock nearby.

He pulled off his leather jacket and draped it around my shoulders. It caught me by surprise, and I blushed. "It's a little chilly," he said with a timid smile "I won't need it."

Then he tugged off his black knit sweater, revealing his bare chest. I turned away as blood further flushed my cheeks, and I then turned back toward him, to not seem too awkward. The moonlight illuminated his stark, pale chest. He wasn't skinny like some boys our age were. His muscles were well-defined. The fire's light also showcased his features. Swallowing hard, I snapped out of it. Wait, why did he take off his shirt?

From the corner of my eyes, I saw something darting towards me. A tall, slender man and he was also... shirtless? The second he stood above me, I recognized him. A large dragon tattoo on his arm met my face as he stood within inches of Kris.

His blue eyes pierced through me with the fire that danced behind him. It was Valentin. He pointed at me without discretion. Rude much? On the same arm with the dragon tattoo, his fist clenched. An awkward tension rose through the air as Kris stared back at him without fear.

"It's fine. She's my girlfriend." Kris inched between us, protecting me. *Girlfriend?!* I didn't know that!

Given the circumstances, I decided to remain silent. Kris told me I was with him for the initiation. Was that what he meant? Valentin's face contorted in annoyance. Kris's answer didn't seem to appease him.

"Only elite members can come to these gatherings, and you bring a complete stranger." He swung his finger towards me.

I dared to look up and saw the fangs on Valentin's teeth as he talked to Kris. They were not normal. Along with his sharp jawline and rugged five-o'clock shadow, he had a set of fangs? Were those real? Kris stuck his face boldly into his.

"Who is the leader of these meetings, anyway? Is it you, Valentin? Well?" Though Kris was strong for his age he didn't compare to Valentin's stature.

"*Who*?" Valentin countered Kris with rage-filled eyes.

I reached for my boot to pull out a small switchblade inside it. Even though I was just a helpless teen girl compared to him, I wouldn't go down without a fight. Then, a voice boomed from behind the man.

"Valentin." Alex stood behind him, his feet planted, and with a look of power that overshadowed him. "Sit down, Valentin. She is fine," he stated again with an edge of authority to his tone.

I stayed hidden behind Kris with whatever safety he could offer. Valentin seemed to gather his composure once again and went back to a rock diagonal from us. Blood and fumes were still present in his eyes. A hallowing feeling sunk deep into my chest as I realized that I was a weak lamb among a myriad of wolves. If Kris wasn't here, what could I do to protect myself?

"Fellow creatures of the night," Alex's voice echoed among the clan, causing each member's head to turn towards him.

His long black shirt stretched as he raised his hands towards the sky, and his dark piercing eyes met mine. I looked away as fear seeped into my bones.

Kris clenched my hand tighter; he could tell I was afraid. I looked back up at him as questions filled my mind. I knew stuff like this had to exist in the world, but I didn't expect to be here.

"We are here for the baptism," Alex continued, beginning to circle the bonfire. "Dayton, Hexane, come up."

Two dark-clad men raced to the middle of the circle. Alex raised his arm towards us.

"Kris," his voice called to him, and Kris stood up to join the two men.

A proud look came upon Alex's face as Kris walked over. They all stood in a line and dropped to their knees in one synonymous motion. Kris glanced up at me with a knowing glimmer in his eyes.

Alex whispered in what seemed to be another language, then grabbed one of the lit torches. In one swift moment, he whisked away and lit the small silver cross in front of the three bowing men.

"Renounce Christ," he stated firmly

"We renounce Christ." the three chanted in unison.

"Be baptized in fire." Alex removed the cross from the fire and pressed it onto the first man's neck. The man cringed and then raised his head solemnly. Alex continued with the next man.

My heart thundered in my chest. Was he going to do this to Kris?

I twinged on the inside. Why? Why would he do that? Kris turned his face towards me as Alex approached him. He smiled at me with the calmest face I had ever seen.

I clenched the edge of Kris's leather jacket sleeve as Alex pressed the cross onto Kris's neck. I pulled my own hand to my neck in disbelief. How could he do that? Within a moment he looked back up at me with a straight face despite the pain I knew he was in. My blank expression matched his across the fire's flames between us. His face remained the same with just one tear streaked across his cheek.

The three men all whispered a chant. The wind howled and swayed the surrounding flames. I sensed a shift in the atmosphere, almost like a sigh amongst the clan. Kris and the other two men stood up with their heads still down.

Clan members gathered around Kris and Alex. Zayn walked towards Kris. She put her hand on his shoulder and glanced back over at me, and we caught each other's gaze. It was over. A sense of relief ran through me.

I quickly stared back at the fire. I didn't want to appear nervous and remained seated on the stone that Kris had originally guided me to. My arms trembled as a chill hit my face, making the bonfire flames wave. Kris stopped talking to the man in front of him and returned to me. I gave him a meek smile.

"Dalia, this is Dayton." He pointed to the other guy now towering over me. Why was everyone here so tall?

"Hi," I replied, standing up to shake his hand. My petite frame put me in front of his large bare chest. Why were they okay with being shirtless in this air?

Dayton nodded at me confidently.

"He is a long-time friend of mine. Like a brother," Kris continued, nodding towards me. "And this is my friend, Dalia."

"Aren't you cold?" I whispered to Kris. His brow furrowed as he laughed.

"It's worth it to get initiated." He shrugged and pulled his shirt back on

This was all strange... and interesting. I would need Kris to tell me more on the way home. The silence must have stretched too long as Kris changed the subject.

"Well, Congratulations!" He patted Dayton on the shoulder. "I need to take Dalia home now." Kris reached to take my hand, and I gladly placed mine in his. His chivalry left me enamored by him.

We stumbled through the trees and back to his car. He swooped away some of his hair to show me the burn on his neck, in the form of an upside-down cross.

"I like it." I grinned.

The ride home was nothing less than awkward.

"So, what did you think?' he questioned me eagerly.

"I thought I was watching a cult horror movie scene, but in real life."

He smiled a little and looked nervously at me. I was being honest.

"I wanted you to see a part of me. A part of my world. The group is family to me." he explained.

I could see that he was honest about who he was. The only thing that made him alive was the clan. Just like when I cut myself, I felt alive. I guess my soul was just like his. Kris sped down the secluded suburban streets. The traffic had waned, and we were alone as he parked in front of my house.

"It's not a goth club, but it's a home," I remarked thoughtfully.

He nodded with a smile. But it didn't seem to amuse him. I slowly reached for the door handle, and then Kris jumped. His quick movements startled me.

"Let me get it for you," he insisted as he hurried out of the car.

I never had anyone be so kind. He opened the door for me as I got out of the car. I paused for a moment in front of him as he slammed the door shut. Out of the corner of my eye, I noticed a slight rustle in the front dining room window curtain.

I rolled my eyes and looked at Kris. "My dad." I smiled sheepishly at him.

"He should be overprotective with a daughter like you," Kris replied. "I'll watch you walk to the door to make sure you make it there alive."

"I can fend for myself," I answered with a note of sarcasm.

"We'll see about that." he teased.

I leaned in closer to his face. "You have no idea."

Of course, my dad chose that moment to pop his head out the front door.

"Dalia?" His voice sounded stern.

"One second, Dad," I sighed, glancing one last time at Kris as I backed away. "I've got to go."

"See you tomorrow?" Kris inquired.

"Tomorrow." I nodded.

As I stumbled up the steps to our quaint little home, I turned back for just one second. Kris mesmerized me. At least until I had to turn around and explain to my dad why I wasn't with Elise, but with a boy instead. My dad looked at me conspicuously, raising an eyebrow as he waited for me to speak.

"It's ok, Dad! It's just a guy that I met. He is new to town, and I became his friend." I shrugged, trying to sound casual.

"Get rest for tomorrow," he ordered as I walked towards my bedroom door.

When I closed the door to my bedroom, I pulled out my laptop. I had some research to do and typed *vampire clans* into my web browser. Thousands of websites came up; some were even unpronounceable. Names that sounded medieval, ancient, and eccentric. I would have to narrow this search to 'vampire clans New Orleans'. I clicked on the first thing that popped up. A black screen filled the page with the word 'NOVA' across the top. Red letters unfolded the acronym. New Orleans Vampire Association. I scrolled down to just see what looked like a group of goths that loved to go clubbing. And on rare occasions, they did charity events, *and* they owned a bookstore. Surely, this wasn't the mysterious clan Kris was in?

Something scrolled past my page. An ad for ...a bookshop? *"Boutique Du Vampyre."* Red font scrawled across the page. Maybe Kris was not my only way to discover the truth about the clan? I had to find out more.

Chapter Fourteen
Relentless

THE INITIATION WAS SEARED into my mind like the upside-down cross on Kris's neck. In turn, my thoughts burned with questions. Where did the vampire clan start? I considered myself an expert on vampires, but what happened last night was out of my scope of knowledge. Maybe they were something else? The clan was a whole new world to me. Sleeping in coffins, drinking blood, and crazy rituals in the woods were typical. But having an inverted cross seared onto your neck?

Traditionally, vampires were repelled by crucifixes. Beyond that was the fact that they derived their beliefs from the bible. The night I was at the Batcave replayed in my mind. Kris's broad shoulders and well-toned stature. His enchanting demeanor, his lips, and eyes that caused my heart to betray my body as he pulled out the old bible and quoted, *"Life is within the blood."*

Those words somehow rang true to my spirit. They became etched within me, causing me to long for more. I scanned myself one last time in the mirror above my vanity. Kris brought me to see things that I could never unsee. The high-pitched beep of

Elise's Volkswagen jolted me. I scrambled to pick up my bag and phone. Looking up in the mirror for a second, I gazed deep into my eyes once again. Was I a person like Kris? Could I be part of the clan too?

Hurrying outside the house, I slipped into the passenger seat next to Elise. Biting my lip as she started driving, I finally blurted, "I need to ask you a favor... please."

Her eyes widened as she glanced at me from the wheel. "Huh What?" Her expression seemed like she hadn't fully woken up yet.

"Can you drive me downtown?" I asked.

"Again?" she groaned.

"Please. It's Friday. I've spent a whole week at treatment, and I was hoping we could skip today for this,"

She grunted. "Do we have to go *now*?" Her face looked puzzled.

"I need to go to this place." I handed her a paper with the words scratched across it *Boutique du Vampire* and an almost illegible address on it. She stared back up at me.

"Why? Is this something to do with Kris?" Elise asked, raising a brow.

"Kind of. I'm looking for answers about him. Please." I reiterated.

A heavy sigh blew from her lungs. "Anything for my friend. But you owe me an extra movie night together."

"Promise!" I chimed.

My hands shook with the eagerness welling up inside me. Elise rushed up behind me after slipping two quarters into the parking meter.

"Thank you, Elise." My eyes sheepishly acknowledged her struggle to come along with me.

A large hanging wooden sign carved with the words *Boutique du Vampire* on it faced me as I opened the door. I gazed at every inch of the boutique, eagerly taking everything in. Large Voodoo doctor masks were plastered across a wooden wall. Coffin-shaped purses, gothic jewelry, clothes, and even custom snacks stocked the shelves. An enormous wine bottle labeled '*Vampire Blood*' sat on one shelf. *That's ironic!* I wondered if this was the clan's wine supplier.

Other items labeled vampire tea, vampire... hot sauce? I grimaced. Even though I was born and raised in New Orleans, I still never acclimated my tastes to its spicy food. Incense rose from the checkout counter where I also spotted a small altar to a Voodoo god. Next to the altar, a petite woman with hot pink hair hid behind a magazine. Why hadn't I visited this place before? Maybe because it was downtown, and my parents didn't want to fuel my vampire obsession. Skipping rehab was definitely worth it.

I turned to scan the store again and found the spot I was searching for. Elise was busy studying Voodoo masks, so I slipped over to the shelves of books lined on a large black, wooden bookshelf. Not just any books; vampire books. I. Was. In. Heaven. Hours could escape me here, just reading and admiring every book.

Wait, Dalia! Focus. I was just looking for one thing here.

"Nova, Nova..." My finger brushed the "M-P" section on the bottom shelf. Nothing relative to it. I jumped up to the section for books in "C" only to see nothing about vampire clans. My fingers lingered on the spine of a book, my brows furrowing.

"Can I help you with something?" A voice behind me made me jump. "Elise?" But it wasn't Elise. It was the girl from the counter.

Her eyes held an intensity to them that made me shiver slightly. Bright pink hair framed a flawless complexion with rounded cheeks, pierced eyebrows, and dark brown eyes. I glanced at the front of the store. Kris moved in the same level of silence as her.

"What can I help you with today?" She had a southern draw to her voice.

"Oh, I'm just looking around. I've never been here before." I shrugged, offering a polite smile.

Her smile faded. "Have you read this before?" She pulled out a large leatherbound book that looked more like an encyclopedia.

"No. I haven't." I reached for the book and held it in my hands like the holy grail. *'Vampire Encyclopedia'* it read on the front of the cover. Oh, one of these. Almost like the Gunness Book of World Records. I rolled my eyes, but not enough to let the girl see.

"Great, thank you." I flipped through the pages to show I was interested.

She walked towards Elise at the front counter to check her out. What did she expect me to find? I glanced at the preface in the book's front page. Egypt. The Middle East. Romania. Eastern Europe. Dracula. I paused for a second and ruffled through the pages. One page had a large crucifix on it with the title 'Weapons against the ancient vampire.' That's what I thought. I didn't know what to think of Kris's vampire traditions. I thought vampires were repelled by the crucifix. If anything, it seemed like they were drawn to it.

A black flyer suddenly fell out of the book onto the floor. My brows furrowed. I picked it up off the red cement floor. Words were printed in classic black metal text, *'NOVA'*. A man with a white-painted face, black lips, and eyes pictured on the front. I glanced back up towards Elise. She was chatting with the pink-haired lady. She always had a way of striking up a conversation with anyone. I pushed the book back onto the shelf but held onto the flyer.

"Elise," I interrupted the conversation after walking over. The girl with pink hair smiled at me again. I glanced at the girl.

"Do you know about this?' I raised up the flyer.

"Oh! That's a concert happening around here." She glanced at a calendar by the counter. "Tonight actually."

"Really?" I paused and looked at Elise.

"Yeah, you should come out. Many vampire folklore lovers are into NOVA's music."

I nodded and slipped the flyer into my pocket. Two sharp fangs peeked out of her black-lined lips, ones I hadn't noticed before. She had to be part of the clan.

"I think we need to go," I replied and glanced at Elise, to not look suspicious.

"Awe! Hate to see you leave! Would you like to pick out a magazine?" The girl pointed at the rows of tattoo, BDSM, and 'Modern Wicca' magazines below her counter. "It will be my treat."

Elise's eyes widened in delight. She could never pass up a freebie. She snatched a 'vegan goth' magazine from the bottom row. "Thank you!" she exclaimed.

I tugged on her hand. "Thank you so much! We have to go now!" I walked back outside with Elise in tow.

"Why the hurry?" She questioned as I led her out the door.

I peered inside the window for a second. The girl with pink hair had her face hidden by the magazine she was reading again. Maybe I was wrong.

"I think she may be part of the clan. I didn't want to stay too long."

Elise pulled a face. "Part of the clan?"

"Yes." I replied with a nod.

"I don't know, Dalia. She seemed fine to me," she stated naive-ly.

"It's just..." I raised my hand up slightly. I didn't want her to have the slightest doubt that what I was getting into wasn't safe. But there was Valentin. I never told her about him. I had to think of something.

"I don't want Kris to think I'm stalking him or something like that."

"Maybe you are," Elise chuckled and nudged my side.

I immediately felt stricken with guilt. Blood rushed to my head. Gosh. She may be right. Thankfully, it was October and not June and I could withstand the extra sweating this conviction gave me.

"Hey, are you okay, Dalia?" she asked. Her steps became even more bouncy.

"I'm fine,' I replied with a stillness in my voice, trying to brush off the jarring reality Elise may have pointed out. I didn't want to think of myself as a stalker. "Elise, do you think we could go to this concert tonight?'

"Would this help you find out more about the clan?" she replied softly. Maybe she was prying. She must have sensed there was more I wasn't telling her. I glanced down at the pavement on the sidewalk. "Possibly," I mumbled as we turned the corner to find her car.

"We can go, Dalia. Even for that reason. It would be fun!" she chimed.

We walked down the street to our parking meter which stood beside small hedges surrounding a property until my eyes caught a small white cross. It was similar to the cross on Kris's neck. What was the significance of the cross? The crucifix was planted in the middle of the garden surrounding the chapel. A figure carved to look like Jesus hung upon it. His face and eyes were serene, though the monument was worn and weathered.

I caught a sign before it that read, '*St. Steven's Chapel*'. I think I would die or even go up in flames before stepping foot into a church. At least I was honest enough to admit that I knew my soul was wicked.

Mom took me to a couple of Sunday services on holidays. Easter, Christmas, stuff like that when I was younger. There were always gray-haired old ladies who pinched my cheeks and meekly asked if I knew about Jesus. It had been years since I stepped foot in a church, and I doubted that their reaction to me would be the same as when I was younger.

After Elise nearly crashed the car downtown maneuvering the streets packed with tourists and stopped by a gas station, we decided to grab some lunch. Elise and I trailed into the rickety cafe acting as if we were old enough to not be at school and trailed our way into an adventure this morning. The cafe was filled with the aroma of coffee and tomato bisque soup. We both sat at an empty black booth by a bright window.

"So... you never filled me in. How did it go last night?" Elise asked with a grin. "Did a vampire guy keep you up late?"

I shrugged. "I guess it's harder than I thought to be a creature of the night. Aside from what you're thinking, it was interesting, to say the least. Kris brought me to an initiation into the clan that his uncle leads."

Her face twinged a bit, indicating how uncomfortable my response made her. I quickly placed my hand over hers.

"It's fine," I tried to comfort her. A couple of book nerds close by stuck their noses out of their manga and glimpsed at Elise's stricken face. "I'm trying to be on the down low about this!"

A petite waitress came up to the table and laid a couple of menus out, snapping both of us out of our moment.

"We both want water," I said before the girl could ask her first routine question.

She plastered on a smile. "I'll be right back," she said in a high-pitched tone.

"Dalia, are you sure that it's safe for you to hang out with him? I mean, you have no idea what the clan really does or gets into." Elise was flooded with questions again. My memory raced back to how Kris defended me in front of Valentin. The angry clan member was about to beat my face in last night.

"Elise, I feel safe with Kris." I looked deep into her eyes and then over at a table of middle-aged men talking loudly. They were immersed in a heated game of D&D.

"Are you sure? I mean, you didn't seem like that just a minute ago at the bookstore." Her face scrunched with uncertainty.

I nodded, giving her a serious look. "I'm positive." My hand was on hers still. "I know I'm safe with Kris."

Even though I put forth confidence with Elise and tried to rationalize things myself, I knew that Elise's and my emotions collided. Was I safe with Kris?

Chapter Fifteen

Songs for Rain

I LACED UP THE corset straps on my black tattered dress. Deep red hues lined the seams and flowers were embroidered between the corset bones. This was the closest I got to wearing color. I let my long black hair down to cover my shoulders and finished off everything with a deep red lipstick. My hope was that I wouldn't run into anyone from the clan tonight. If I did, my second wish would be that they wouldn't recognize me. I pulled out my small knife with the handle in the shape of a dragon and tucked it into the side of my left boot. I *also* hoped that I didn't have to use this tonight.

"I've got to go, Dad. Elise is here!" I yelled by his door before running down the hallway.

The clan wasn't the only thing I was trying to avoid tonight. A silent hand suddenly grabbed my shoulder with an air of authority. I turned to face my dad.

His eyes traveled to my tattered fishnet stockings and combat boots. "Be safe out there."

"Don't worry Dad, I will." I embraced him firmly under the arm he stopped me with, surprised he didn't ask me to change before leaving. Then I finished sprinting outside to the waiting Volkswagen on the curb.

"About time," Elise remarked as I opened the passenger door. She eyed me like my dad did.

"You look like a vampire queen. Are you nervous?"

"No," I replied, glancing out the window. "I would be more nervous if I were you."

"Why me?" She startled and looked down at herself in confusion.

She had a pale blue lace top, denim bell bottoms, and jeweled sandals. An opal gemstone necklace hung below her neck and her wavy blonde hair flowed past her shoulders.

Elise made a face and shrugged. "I guess you're right. If it's a vampire concert, I'm gonna stand out in the crowd tonight," she amended.

"It's okay, you can be a vampire at Woodstock!" I chuckled.

Elise laughed at my compliment, turned on some John Lennon for the drive, and started the lengthy trip downtown. Staring at each house and building go by, I reflected on last night again. My knees were shaking, and my heart racing. If any other clan member just happened to be there tonight, and I was without Kris, it could be deadly. I must be on alert. The cold from the blade tucked into my boot reminded me what it was there for.

When we reached the French Quarter, Elise sandwiched her car into a parking space with a meter across from our destination, *The Door Club*. The air of a typical southern fall met me as I looked across the street to the line of young goths, emos, and punks waiting outside the venue. I could survive the brisk air even if I dressed in all black. I glanced at Elise as she walked with a little skip in her step. In her baby-blue denim, she stood out just as much as I did, but in a different way. It was intimidating to even walk up, but I tried not to be too awkward standing there as we waited to get in.

Why was I here? I checked my options again. I was here to find out more about the clan. There had to be some reason they titled the concert "NOVA". Could it be that the clan used events like this as another secret way to gather? Possibly to recruit people for blood donations?

"Let's go." I grabbed Elise's hand and started walking inside when it was our turn.

The club was just as dark as I imagined. It was like walking into a large black box. The walls, floor, and ceiling were all painted a deep onyx. The only thing that contrasted the darkness was the bar in the middle of the room and small tables lined around the walls with light bulbs hanging above. Elise wrapped her tiny hand around my elbow; she must be as nervous as I was. I scanned the room for the best corner, chair, or wall we could stand by. Any place that we wouldn't be too noticeable to clan members. Going to the Batcave gave me some experience with this kind of stuff. Some empty chairs by steel tables were close to the front of the stage. The corner was shrouded in darkness by the wall and a corner in contrast to the blinding stage lights.

"Let's sit at those tables." I pointed toward them to show Elise. We both sat close to the wall. It was the safest place and out of the way of any concertgoers.

"I need to go to the bathroom real quick," Elise stammered, looking sheepish as she got up.

"Wait! I should go with you." I stopped her, and Elise nodded.

We traveled across the room to a deep red hallway. The doors to the bathroom were scuffed up with band stickers plastered randomly all over them.

"I'll wait out here," I told her, standing by the door as she went inside. I didn't want to see the quality of the bathrooms, and this would give me a chance to see if I recognized any clan members in the room yet.

The couple of faces I saw were unrecognizable. I studied the bar, seeing only a couple of young girls in band tees sitting next to some guys with the same attire. No Valentin, Vivid, or even the Elvira 2.0 that watched the door at the Batcave. The crowds that started to congregate by the stage didn't look like any clan members either. When Elise returned, we traveled back to the tables as I looked around to see if I saw anyone familiar. Anyone at all.

As far as I could tell, normal young adult partygoers filled the concert floor. I looked down at my watch, seeing it was already 10 p.m. The crowd cheered as soft melodies vibrated the venue at every note.

A girl dressed in all black sang, swaying behind the microphone. She looked beautiful and reminded me of a younger version of Zayn. NOVA strummed the sounds from the guitar, bass, and even an electric keyboard. Their music reminded me of an early 80s new wave band. Light and elusive tones mixed with guitar. At the very least, I could enjoy the music tonight, and hopefully go home and be at peace knowing nothing happened to Elise or myself. I watched contentedly as the girl sang the hallowed tunes until light shadows crossed her face. Something moving from above startled me. The beams for the stagehands in the concert venue shook.

I turned towards the girl singing but out of curiosity looked up again. A man stood up on the beams above me, making my blood run cold. His eyes grabbed my soul as he stood there staring down at me. He held a stark white face and black beaming eyes. Maybe if I ignored him, he would stop staring at me. Why wasn't he looking at the band on stage instead?

Again, I looked up to the balcony and shuddered. He still was staring right at me. And he wasn't alone this time. A tall older man with a trench coat draped over his body accompanied him. As I watched, his eyes met mine again. Maybe they recognized me from the initiation? I grabbed Elise's arm. She was still bobbing her head to the music, oblivious to what was happening. I panicked and shouted over the music to her.

"We have to go." I hurriedly pulled her from the bar chairs.

"Now?" she yelled back, her eyebrows furrowing in confusion.

"Just trust me!" I pressed.

She put her handmade yarn satchel over her arm and took my hand. We squeezed through the crowd and made it to the back of the venue. I looked out past the sea of people and towards the door of the concert hall. A heavy gasp escaped my lungs as we made it out of the venue's narrow door and to the sidewalk we waited in line at.

"What is going on? What happened?" Elise stammered, trying her best to keep up with me as I walked towards her car.

"We just—" I continued to cross the street. "We have to go."

Elise followed as we dodged the couple cars driving by and crossed the intersection.

'What is going on, Dalia?" she repeated, more urgently this time.

I grabbed Elise by the shoulders. "If you want to go home in one piece, we need to leave now."

Her eyes widened. I may have said too much, but I couldn't help it in my panicked state.

After hopping back in the car, her beetle sputtered away from the venue, and I sunk into the passenger seat, relieved that nothing happened to us. Elise concentrated on navigating the downtown traffic and not crashing. Even though I've watched a million horror movies, the man's eyes chilled me to the bone. Why was he standing above me and staring at me? He had to have been a clan member who recognized me. I pulled my arms over my shoulders to hug my body. I was safe now. Or was I just overreacting?

"Do you think what you were experiencing was just another panic attack?" Elise's eyes trailed down to my arm as I pressed it close to my torso, but I shook my head.

"It's not what you think. I'm fine." How do I tell her about Valentin? My heart throbbed. Was I so desperate to do anything to find answers? What I did know was something happened that I cannot explain. Not even to Elise. But I didn't want to raise her fears about Kris or the clan. We turned a corner as Elise frantically tinkered with her GPS. The red lights from the Batcave passed by my window. Maybe Kris was still inside?

"Elise, can you stop here?" I asked hesitantly, and she balked at me. "I'm serious. Stop. "

She slammed on the brakes and swerved to the side of the street, skidding by another car. Her face was exasperated as she parked by the sidewalk.

"Elise, I'm sorry. I have to go see Kris." I opened the passenger door and jumped out.

"*What*? What are you doing?" A bead of sweat ran from her forehead down to her furrowed brows.

"I'm so sorry. Can I explain later?' I spoke down to her inside the car.

"I'm going home." She shook her head and drove off.

I lifted my heavy combat boot-covered feet as fast as I could down the busy downtown street. My mind raced with thoughts about the clan again and what Kris would be doing tonight. Could it have been a clan member watching me at the concert? Perhaps Valentin?

Flashing red letters above the Batcave met my eyes once again. My hand touched the black door handle. What if Kris wasn't here? Or he didn't want to see me? I stopped and tugged my bat wing backpack under my arm. I...can't. I cowered to my fears and retreated to the other side of the sidewalk. Maybe I should have let Elise take me home? Where could I go now?

A sudden thud caused me to stop and pulled me out of my thoughts. My face planted right into a black shirt covering a hard, muscular chest. A silver crucifix hung right between my eyes. A narrow face with a demented grin displayed a set of fangs, familiar blue eyes gleaming in the night. He was too close for comfort.

"Look what the bat dragged in," he drawled with a toothy grin. "Too bad Kris isn't here to see this."

"Valentin?" I clenched my fists, ready to swing if needed as he inched closer to me. "Look, I don't know what problem you have with me. But I'm only interested in seeing Kris."

Valentin seemed even more confident than the evening of the initiation. His stature towered over mine, and he wasn't backing away.

"Is that so?" he replied in a mocking tone.

"Yes. In fact, I'm about to call Kris now." My hand shook as I scrolled through my I-watch.

Please let this work. I searched through my contacts. But I didn't even have Kris's number?! Valentin looked down at me with a smirk.

"Don't worry, doll. I'm not buying it." He nudged my arm away.

I stepped back until I hit the club's cement wall. I swung my fist full force towards his face. He turned his head out of the line of fire and laughed.

"Do you want to be a sacrifice?" He put his face inches from mine.

I narrowed my eyes. "Sacrifice?" I demanded.

Valentin pointed to the crucifix hanging around his neck. "Life is in the blood, and your blood smells like it would be sweet." A jagged fingernail swept across my cheek. "You may not know all there is to the clan."

My breath caught until I remembered what Kris told him at the initiation. I could put up a front of having some relation to Kris. With that, I could protect myself.

"Kris loves me. He wouldn't," I blurted out. It sounded stupid, and I wasn't even sure if that was the truth.

Valentin stepped back immediately. Instead of the look of defeat I had hoped for, he let out a loud cackle. I just stood there, unsure of what to think. How could he be so disrespectful? So crazy? Then he turned from a jokester to holding a cold stare. His eyes held murder within them as he moved closer to me until he was mere inches away. I could feel him breathing in my air. My body. My blood. Every second that passed, I felt energy seeping from my being. Pure terror rose within me as I froze against the wall.

"Don't be so sure of love, Dalia." He swiftly turned with that last remark. His blood-red trench coat swayed as he walked around the corner to enter the Batcave.

Every muscle within my body let go of the tension held inside. *He's gone now.* I turned in each direction, searching for a way out of here. The streets were unforgivingly empty around me. Sweat—no, tears—trickled down my face, and I rubbed it away. Did I not even know that I cried? I released every emotion and began to run. I needed to go to the graveyard.

Chapter Sixteen

Graveyard Encounter

A THUNDERSTORM BREWED IN the distance with heavy clouds. Below the expanse of darkness, a weathered tombstone in the shape of a cross by the graveyard's wrought-iron gate made me shudder. It reminded me of the crucifix on Valentin's necklace and the upside-down cross from the initiation. I clutched onto the iron bars separating me from the graves. What did Valentin mean by sacrifice? Why was the crucifix so significant to the clan? Fear gripped my body as I pushed through the cemetery's gate. Did they intend to make me a sacrifice?

'Life is within the blood, and yours smells sweet.' Valentin's words hissed through my thoughts. They reminded me of Kris but in a twisted way.

Why was Valentin out to get me, anyway? Yet another question that only Kris could answer. I retreated to the cemetery's gazebo. The only safe place I knew of right now. The large cement structure had been here since I first discovered Lafayette cemetery. It kept all my memories trapped inside of it, good and bad. It was the prison of my dreams, as I read one vampire novel after another. Imagining myself in another life where I was a vampire. The gazebo was like a coffin itself. Locked up within the stone walls with death all around me. I set my black leather backpack on the ground next to a small corner in the gazebo. Behind a terrace with vines, I hid a stack of books with a votive and lighter.

I sat down and lit the small white votive, casting shadows across the gazebo walls as the subtle breeze caused the flame to dance and flicker. Though I survived the encounter with Valentin, I could not escape him forever. My anxiety, a tightness in my chest, wouldn't let that reality go. I pulled my hand into my bag and checked around to make sure Elise had not followed me to the graveyard. She wouldn't like what I was about to do. A small mint container held a blade inside my backpack. It gleamed with promise as I pulled it out. My heart ached for what calmed me in these moments.

I closed my eyes as I slid the blade across my arm, digging into my flesh. Pain was my only comfort as tears came up along with the blood. As the blade sunk deep, the truth came to my mind again. That there was really no point to life. I lived for another release and etched another slit on my arm. Punishment was my only solution. Another tear streaked down my cheek as I laid my forehead into my hand. Blood trailed down my arm. I looked over the beam separating me between the gazebo and the field of tombstones.

'Don't be so sure of love.' Valentin's taunting voice echoed in my thoughts.

He was right. I still desired to die, but the only thing that made me feel alive or okay with life was love. My arm bled for a couple more minutes until I bunched my sweater sleeve onto the wound. Breathing in the humid cemetery air, I picked a book from my hidden stack behind the terrace and calmed myself by reading a vampire novel. The book caressed my soul as I read:

'She looked across the graveyard before her, filled with bones, the writhing souls in eternal pain. Amongst the graves, a tall, ominous figure appeared. He was with her. She grasped the tomb's ledge as he walked toward her. His glowing red eyes matched the vibrancy of the moon above him. With every inch he moved forward, it was apparent she was never alone.'

A crinkling of leaves behind me caused me to startle. I slammed the book shut and turned to check behind me. My heart jumped in my chest. Kris's dark eyes met mine. He was kneeling down to my level, balancing himself on the tip of his combat boots, crouched over like Batman looking over Gotham City with an amused smile drawn across his face.

"I'm sneaky, aren't I?" He laughed. My body sunk into the gazebo floor as I tried to catch my breath.

"I thought it might have been..." I stopped; I didn't want him to know about my run-in with Valentin yet. Who knew what his reaction would be? I finished, "Elise. She knows this is my secret hideout."

He tenderly stroked his thumb from my temple and tucked a strand of hair behind my ear. Electricity traveled through me. A wave of emotion overcame my being. My arms, my knees, my entire body melted. On his knees, he leaned into me, with his face unusually close to mine. Was he going to kiss me? Devil knew I desired it.

"Well, it's just you and me now," he whispered. Fangs peeked out from his lips as he spoke. His teeth were sharp? I never noticed that before. He stared deep into my eyes and placed his hand on my bleeding arm. With a soft touch, his thumb began to trace the cut beneath my sweater sleeve.

"You don't have to do that alone," he whispered. I clenched my sweater sleeve in my hand. Would he accept and understand why I did this? I pulled myself away from his tender eyes.

"Did you see me walking here?" I interrogated.

"No." He pointed to a tomb nearby with a shrug. "I find the graveyard relaxing. Come." He pulled my better arm, forcing me to trust his every move. His eyes glowed in the moonlight as he led me out of the gazebo and to a single tombstone.

"This is what we have at the end of our lives." He stared longingly at the grave until I placed my hand into his and squeezed it tightly to express my sympathy.

"The graveyard gives me comfort too. It gives me hope that the pain in this life will end." I let the wind cross my face, breathing in deep as I spoke.

Could I stay in this moment forever? Kris holding my hand with the same passions that I had? He was a suffering soul, just like myself. For the first time in ages, I found myself at rest. Feeling my life leak from the wound on my arm, and finding myself with Kris. I realized he was my peace. More than cutting and more than death, I wanted a life with him. I stood in that peace with him, until a question flooded my mind, one that I could not answer. What is so different about *him?*

"Kris, why do I feel so connected to you?" I interjected in the quiet moment between us. The compulsion to curiosity overtook me.

"Your eyes," he said after a moment. "Yes, your eyes. They are so intriguing to me." He led me to a bench next to the gazebo. "I wanted to know more about you. Dalia, people here aren't like you. You're different."

I breathed in with a candid smile. "You think I haven't figured that out by now?" I let my defenses down about him and leaned back on the bench.

Kris wasn't the guy he usually portrayed. He was open, and he had a divine interest in me. His nails were painted black, and a small silver snake ring hung loose on his ring finger. It had beautiful red gemstone eyes. His hand, still within mine, was pale and stark in contrast to his black jeans he laid them on.

"Dalia, what do you believe in?" he interrupted our silence this time.

I could get lost forever just studying details about him. I softly pulled my hand from his. His question was challenging, as I didn't know what I believed about this life.

"I'm not sure. What do you mean?" I replied, furrowing my brows. It seemed rude, but I didn't know what to say.

"What do you think happens after we die?' He pointed to the gravestone near the gazebo.

"I think we rot in the ground in a cemetery that freaks like us hang out in." My answer fell out of my mouth immediately. It was almost instinctual.

He then looked directly into my eyes with a timid smile. "Aside from that, you never answered my first question." Kris continued, "What do you believe in?" I truly didn't know how to answer this.

I clenched my teeth as the thoughts rolled through my mind. I didn't know if there was a god, and if there was, did he care at all? I sighed and turned towards the crucifix across the graveyard by the old wire cemetery gate. What *did* I believe in? A jet-black crow glided from a nearby tree and landed on top of the cross. Reels from The Crow flashed through my head. I had my answer.

"If I believe in anything besides death, I would say I believe in an eternal love." I finally said.

His entire countenance changed. "I want to tell you about the love that I have found. I've found a power and a life that surpasses death." Did this have to do with the clan? This was the most transparent I had ever seen him before. "The clan believes

100

in something that I think would answer many of your questions about death."

"When you die, the worms eat you." I gave him a quirky smile, and the crow cawed from its perch nearby.

"Right. Let me explain what I mean." He laughed. "We believe that you can have eternal life when you go through an initiation. I'm an immortal now. But on this earth—" He stopped mid-sentence as if he were hesitating. Not willing to tell the full truth.

"What?" I pushed him to tell more. The answers I longed to know were on the tip of his tongue.

"When you die as a vampire, you resurrect into a new life, an eternal love." The moonlight shadowed along his complexion as he stared at the empty graveyard. Silence lingered between us for a long moment.

Trying to break that harrowing quiet, I glanced back at my stack of books. "So, vampires aren't only in the stories?" I smirked.

I placed my books into my backpack and stood up beside him. He seemed taken aback by my response. Though his beliefs were intriguing to me, I didn't know if I could believe them.

"Can I take you somewhere?" He turned, changing the tone of his voice.

"Sure," I replied with a smile.

He grabbed his leather jacket hanging over the gazebo railing and placed it over my shoulders. I looked up at him as I blushed.

"It's cold out here." His remark was familiar.

The stories and fantasies locked within my books were not only in my mind. My body flushed with warmth as I smiled. I didn't need to read the vampire romance books. I was living it.

Chapter
Seventeen
United

Kris mounted a large black motorcycle and handed me his helmet. The dark leather seats, enormous wheels, and metallic body made it look expensive. Was his family natural heirs to something? Or did the clan make money from the Batcave?

"Wanna ride?" he asked, and I put a hand over my chest. I'd never ridden a motorcycle, but I've always wanted to.

I calmed myself as I touched the leather seat of the motorcycle. Kris offered his hand to me and lifted me onto the back. I felt his hard chest as I wrapped my arms tightly around him and braced myself for the ride. A blast of air hit my face as he picked up speed. Streetlights turned into faded orbs, and cars became obstacles for Kris to dodge as we skidded along and I clung to Kris for my dear life. When we finally slowed down, we approached a tall iron gate that opened up as he inched closer to it. Kris pulled into the massive driveway. I didn't recognize this place.

"This is my uncle's house," Kris explained.

I stared in awe at the giant house. "Mansion, more like," I added.

Lights inside and outside the home illuminated the property. It was grey, with vines cascading down the front of the house. A large stained-glass window stood front and center above the entrance doors. It could have been a church window with its regal appearance. When you think of a vampire family, you almost expect to see unkept vines, broken statues, and random lightning bolts hitting the roof. Instead, red rose bushes lined the front of the house and the yard was well-maintained. I would bet that had to be Zayn's feminine touch to the home. I still clung onto Kris's waist until he turned towards me with a grin.

"You're free to keep holding on if you like it so much." he teased.

I leaned back and laughed, almost slipping off the back of the bike. He kindly offered his hand as I climbed off the large black motorcycle. Kris didn't let go of my hand as he led me to the front door. The entrance seemed large even for being in a mansion. It reached above ten feet with black iron swirls covering a tinted glass door. He pulled the heavy door open, and I slightly lost my breath. They had decorated the inside in a way I'd always fantasized about for my dream home. Black and red damask walls matched well with deep mahogany wood floors. Long windows hid beneath draping black velvet curtains. Candelabras accentuated the corners of each room, sending flickering light over the interior of the home.

Kris led me into the house and my eyes took in the beauty of it all. We walked into a corridor in the back of the house. An open space with the living room to the left and kitchen to the right. Besides the black walls and deep red furniture or appliances, both appeared normal and functional. No coffins or trap doors.

"Are we the only ones here right now?' I questioned Kris as we walked down a darkened hallway. Kris nodded.

"My uncle should be at the Batcave, and I have something I want to show you."

He stopped before large French doors behind him and held up a large candelabra. It was already lit. Did he plan this? He delicately traced my face, his finger gliding down my jaw, from my ear to my lips.

"Dalia," he whispered delicately, his eyes glowing in the candlelight.

The light cast shadows on him, making him so much more attractive. His prominent cheekbones, soft lips, and jawline stood out all the more. He held his hand in mine as I admired him.

"You don't have to be afraid." He moved his hand onto the small of my back and pulled me closer to him. "What would you like more than anything?" The fierceness of his eyes caused my breath to shallow.

My body tingled from the sensation of his arm around me and his body being so close to mine. I couldn't help but be self-conscious. I wasn't used to this. I needed to divert the conversation. What had I been searching for this whole time? Was it about the clan or about Kris? His face remained the same as he waited for me to respond. I felt the warmth of his body on mine. Wait! I needed to know about the clan.

"I want to live forever, and I want eternal love." I paused, biting my lip, "I want to know more about the clan." I replied bluntly.

Kris stepped back and to my surprise, looked pleased. "What would you like to know?'

I must have had a newfound confidence to be so direct with him. "Where did it start, and where are you really from? I've never seen you or your family in New Orleans before. I've searched books and read millions of vampire novels and have never heard of—"

"Of what?" he interrupted. "A vampire clan?"

104

I was at a loss for words. It was more than just the clan. The crucifix? The sacrifice that Valentin spoke of? Kris began to walk further down the hallway.

"If you have the time, I will answer all your questions. Trust me; you can't find your answers in some vampire book." he drawled.

I followed after him, so as to not be left in the dark.

"Would you like a glass of wine to drink?" He turned to a small wine cellar nearby and took out a bottle. His family wasn't shy about their alcohol, or their blood-drinking habits. "Many members of the clan wouldn't let me give you this." He tilted his head and shrugged.

The concoction in the crystal wineglass looked and smelled much like the drink he gave me the first night at the Batcave. I could only think of Valentin. From that very first encounter, he hated me. Was it because Kris offered me a drink of blood?

"What's the deal with Valentin? He always seems so annoyed at you and at me." I fumbled with my words.

Kris shook his head as he poured out a glass for himself. "He is my cousin."

"Alex's son?"

"Yes, and he likes to get a big head about it. He gets jealous of me sometimes too." Kris shook his head with a smirk.

I was miffed. "Hmm, how so?" I asked. Kris seemed so confident in himself.

He shrugged. "I'm going to be the 'leader of the clan' and he is not."

"So why are you going to lead the clan?"

"You don't think I'm perfect for the role?" Kris's mouth slightly quirked up on one side.

"No, no! It's not that. It's just... I didn't understand." I laughed. "Alex is the clan leader. So why you and not Valentin, his own son?'

Kris looked away with a slight bit of discomfort in his face. As if he had been asked this question before. Or if this matter was the bane of his existence.

"I can explain." He sipped from his glass and placed it on the wine cellar. "Come this way."

He jangled a giant vault-like doorknob on the large French doors. It was in the shape of a glimmering bat. The coolest thing ever. He dragged it open to reveal one thing I loved most. Books. Rows and rows of shelves full to the brim with books.

"A library?" I squeaked.

"Yes." He smiled again. "And not just any library; this is my parents' library."

"Your parents?" I walked down one row of shelves.

The library was majestic, with large wooden walls. An old, rustic smell of dusty books permeated the air. Moonlight shone through a pointed window that nearly reached the ceiling. It added to the peaceful essence inside the library as the light sent shadows between each row of endless books. Darkness filled the space, save for the moonlight billowing in and the candelabra in Kris's hand.

Kris pointed to a portrait on the back wall. It displayed a man and a woman with a strong demeanor that looked like royalty. The man looked just like Kris but without the rugged punk style. His dad wore a black satin shirt and neatly combed hair instead. His mom was gorgeous with a petite nose, lips, and the same eyes Kris had.

"Were your parents part of the clan?" I questioned him as I walked up to the painting.

"They started it," he replied with a nod. Kris pulled out a large deep red book with coppery gold binding from a shelf nearby. "My parents lived in Italy most of their life and died there." His demeanor was solemn as he opened the worn pages. "They had dreams of coming here. My uncle was able to, but they never did."

Sorrow filled his eyes. I placed my hand on his, hoping to comfort him. Kris sat on top of a wooden desk as he continued.

"They started the clan from rogue artists in Italy, coming together to share their passions and desires. Of course, with my dad and uncle. They were sinister enough to start drinking blood. Their beliefs were that it would give them power for eternity. That there was something greater than merely normal life. The arts drew this out of their souls. They found *real* life in the clan."

I sipped from my wine glass. It had a pungent taste, but it was something I could get used to. The blood in my glass brought my mind to the first night at the Batcave. Where did they get the blood we were drinking? What would my blood be to them? Kris mentioned earlier that I didn't have to cut alone. Did he intend to drink my blood? My head spun with thoughts. But the most prevalent question was the one I asked myself most. The quote that both Kris and Valentin had said.

"The first night I went to the Batcave, why did you say, 'Life was in the blood'? Is that something the clan believes?" I asked him.

"Don't we all?" His response almost seemed sarcastic. "Why do you cut yourself, Dalia?" Kris's eyes flashed up to meet mine.

I stirred uncomfortably. Why did he have to ask me that? My heart pounded at the thought of opening up to him about it. But his gaze looked so gentle as he looked at me. He inched closer. I could trust him, I think.

"It reminds me that I'm able to die." I stared down at the floor. "The pain makes me feel alive." I pulled the sleeve on my wounded arm up.

The moonlight hit the part where my cuts were deep, reflecting against the fresh red hues. Kris didn't seem fazed by the response as he came closer to me. His hand gently touched the wounds. Gliding his finger across them as if he could heal them with a simple caress.

"Don't worry, I completely understand," he whispered. "To fully answer your question. Everyone knows that life is within the blood. That is why you cut. It reminds you that you can die. You can only die if you're alive."

I pulled my sleeve back down. I desperately wanted to not talk about cutting anymore. As much as I loved it, I was also severely addicted to the sensation.

"I also saw that quote in the bible." I redirected the conversation.

A smile played on Kris's lips. "My dad took that from the bible. My grandparents were Roman Catholic. They rejected my parents for being heathens."

"Really?" I had no clue about how that worked. Why would someone reject their own child?" I was intrigued.

"Yes, they believed that when you take communion and drink the wine, it turns into Jesus's blood. Silly really, but my dad took it to a whole new level." He looked back at the portrait of his parents, his gaze wistful.

"So, your dad was trying to mock his parents' faith?"

Kris continued admiring the picture, tilting his head in thought.

"I guess so. I think my dad was a genius for what he created. I barely knew him, though. We know we aren't drinking the blood of Jesus. But we do believe the essential truth. Life is within the blood. No matter who it is taken from."

His gaze left the portrait, and he moved closer to me. I didn't step back. I desired for him to take my blood. He could take my life if he wanted. He combed his hand through my hair. His body was so close that I could hear his heart beating rhythmically.

His breath cascaded down my neck. "My mother, she was queen of the clan."

"That's why she looks so regal," I replied.

Kris lifted up my hand and kissed it. His fangs peeked from behind his lips. I tingled from his intoxicating touch.

"I would love for you to be my queen." He drew his face closer to mine. My heart pounded as an electric sensation pulsed through my entire being.

"Dalia, would you like to be part of the clan? Part of me?" he whispered.

I breathed, "Yes, I do. I want to be part of the clan." I put my arms around him, pulling him closer to me.

Could this be my home? Where I belonged was with Kris and the clan. Finally, his lips touched mine with an intoxicating kiss. Life jolted through me as his teeth slightly glided on my lips. He pulled back, and his eyes read into my soul. He was seeing through me. He knew that I desired him completely. He turned my face to the side as the pulse in my neck met his tender lips. He kissed my neck gently.

Every vampire scene from the movies rushed through my mind. His fangs would lengthen as they pierced into my skin. He would fill himself with every last drop of my blood. My body would become limp, my face pale, and I would die in his arms. The beauty of giving myself to him, the vampire, was where I would find myself alive. I would reawaken to immortality. Was this it? Was this when he would take my life?

My face turned towards the tall window with the moonlight seeping in. Rain pattered against the jaded glass, and a roll of thunder outside echoed my feelings for him. This moment was as strong as the thunder. A tear streaked down my cheek. Not because I grieved, but because for the first time, I felt purpose in this life. Kris lifted his lips from my neck and held me tight. The warmth from his body filled my soul.

"I want you completely, Dalia. You can be mine, and I can be yours." His breath beat against my neck as he spoke. My body felt every wave of emotion as he kissed my neck again.

"Dalia, please tell me you feel the way I do for you," he whispered in my ear.

"I do." Thunder clambered by the window as the rain poured against it. The sound became violent and shrouded any silence within the library. I never wanted to leave this place. Our whole bodies, our beings, our souls were united.

Chapter Eighteen

Daggers

I LOOKED UP AT the candle Kris had lit before falling asleep. It was still flickering on the nightstand next to me. The pounding rain and the storm outside matched the storm within me. I heard nothing but the rhythm of the raindrops on the large Victorian window. The red silk sheets covered my body. I turned over to Kris, seeing he was covered too. His chest raised and lowered slowly. Even when he was asleep, he looked so angelic. Perfect and otherworldly.

I slowly raised myself up from the sheets. The cold air blanketed my body instead. I turned to the large dark wooden bedroom door and, noticed a familiar painting across the room next to a tall vanity mirror. The girl in the painting had a perfect frame dressed in a white chiffon dress. It contrasted with the darkness that surrounded her. Her vampire lover held her in his arms. Her neck tilted towards his fangs. Was the girl a precious lover or a victim?

A slight movement from behind me caused me to turn around. Kris lifted out of the sheets. His bare chest peeked out from the stark red, a timid smile crossing his face.

"You're awake." His voice caused a wave of peace to come over me. He uncovered from the sheets.

Electrifying senses overwhelmed my body as I gazed at him. I turned towards the window with the beating rain. I wanted to give him some level of privacy even though I had shamelessly witnessed every part of him last night. I pulled my clothes back on quickly. Looking at him again, I saw he was now dressed in his jeans and a loose T-shirt. He walked over to me. His smoky eyes deepened as he lifted my chin.

"I loved last night." His chest became a heavy tomb as he wrapped his arms around me.

His fingers tucked a strand of hair behind my ear. Along with the rain, I heard his consistent beating heart in his chest. He pulled away, and soft lips met my own. The same electricity flowed through my body once more.

His eyes looked deep into mine. "Do you like my painting?"

"Yes," I replied softly. He pushed up on the bottom of the wooden frame of the painting. Unmounting the painting from the wall and to my surprise, handing it to me.

"You can keep it. To remind you of my love." He leaned in closer. Our eyes had the conversation more than words. "I love you." He placed his hand on my shoulder. "Let me take you home."

Kris stroked my back and arms as he spoke, his lips meeting mine in yet another kiss. His eyes, his everything forged deep within my soul last night. One thing I will never forget. He guided me past the large wooden door, down the hall where we kissed last night in front of the library, through the kitchen, and out of the parlor, until we reached the front door. My heart pounding with every step we took. I looked around, taking in every detail.

Every inch of this place. I will never forget this. I must remember how amazing this all was.

Sitting down in the black leather seat inside Kris's car felt like reality had swept me away. It stole me from the gothic mansion that was my perfect fantasy. Kris held my hand tenderly in his as he drove. I stared out the window in silence. As we approached my neighborhood reality hit me again. Elise?! What happened to her last night after the concert? Kris noticed I had moved my hand.

"Are you okay?" he asked carefully.

I looked down at my phone. She never texted me, called, or anything. Neither did Dad.

"Here." I pointed to the sidewalk close to Elise's house, right around the corner from mine. "You can stop here."

Kris jolted on the brakes. "You sure?"

"Yes," I replied nervously. "It may seem silly, but I don't want my dad to see you dropping me off. He would freak out."

Kris nodded in understanding. I reached for the door handle; everything still felt so surreal.

"Wait!" He stopped me as I began to slip out of the door. "Can I pick you up tonight?" he asked.

"Of course." I smiled as I stumbled out of the car.

"I'll see you soon." His voice echoed.

Kris drove away while I stood silent and breathed in deeply. My eyes closed, and I faced the sky. What just happened last night? My heart fluttered at every moment of last night. Kris holding me close to his heart. His body perfectly embracing mine. The contentment that filled my soul when he kissed me. His eyes glistened in the moonlight from the tall window of their library.

Now I must face reality again. I noted Elise's green Volkswagen parked next to her parents' newer minivan. Should I try to talk to her? I knew that Elise would always understand. If my dad questioned me too much about why I was gone last night, she would always have my back. I pulled out my phone to text her.

"You're okay!" I jumped at the sound of her voice. Elise flung the door open and hugged me tight. I pulled her back and stared directly into her eyes.

"I was kind of worried after your freakout last night, and I thought it might have been because of Kris." She expelled all her words in one long-winded sentence.

I placed my hand on her shoulder, looking in her innocent eyes. "Elise, I'm so sorry."

Her lemonade-smelling locks wisped around my arms as I embraced her. She was my absolute best friend. Guilt filled my heart for how I'd made her feel.

"I'm fine," I assured her. "I ran into Kris at the graveyard last night, and he gave me a ride home." I lied.

Elise looked at the ground and then back up at me. "But is everything going okay with you and Kris? You seemed kind of different last night. What did you see at the concert that made you want to leave?"

"I'm *fine*. Honestly, I just had a slight bit of claustrophobia in the crowded venue last night. I panicked and had to run." I shrugged, feigning nonchalance.

Elise took every word I said with a comforting smile. How did I get to this point? My conscience pulled, and I hesitated to tell her. Could she even understand what Kris told me about the clan? That I was interested in *joining* the clan? I had to cover this up. How could she believe what I was telling her?

"I understand, Dalia." She lightly brushed her hand on mine.

My words had me choked up. Now I was hiding stuff from Elise? How could I explain the details of the clan and even my desire for Kris? Even though he may do the exact opposite of what my vegan hippie friend stood for: drinking human blood.

"Want to go hang out at your place?" she suggested with a meek smile.

"Sure."

My heart melted. I was going to have to sneak out during our movie night. Guilt piled within me again at the thought.

Chapter Nineteen

Fate

ELISE PLUGGED IN THE DVD player and put in Christmas Nightmare as I chugged my monster drink. It was going to be a late night. I pulled out the beautiful portrait that Kris had given me out of my backpack. Holding it up like I had won the Nobel prize, and walked over to my bed, matching the spot that would be perfect for it. I stepped back to observe it again as it hung just above my headboard. Elise knew me too well, and I felt like she could see right through my lies about what was going on. I needed to be honest and tell her how I felt. What really was happening between Kris and I.

"Where did you get that?" She pointed at the painting, furrowing her brows.

"Kris gave it to me," I replied simply.

"At least he is good at art." She peeked in closer to the portrait. "Really good."

I leaned towards her, almost as if I would whisper. "I think I'm in love."

"Are you serious?" She gave me a cold, hard stare, but snapped out of it quickly.

"Elise, I didn't mention this to you, but..." I braced myself for any reaction. "Kris likes me too. He told me last night." I almost halfway cringed, just hoping she wouldn't be mad.

"That's great, Dalia. I'm happy for you," she said stiffly.

She bent over to start the DVD player. I sensed her reaction wasn't genuine. Maybe she would grow to love him? Once she saw what I saw in Kris.

"Are you sure, Elise?" I said cautiously.

She nodded with a smile.

"Thank you." I hugged her and sat next to her on my bed. I wasn't going to push her anymore today.

Christmas Nightmare played across the screen. The classic that warmed my heart. The scene when they realized he was meant to be with Sarah made me think of myself with Kris. Last night would never be forgotten. When he kissed me, I realized just how much I love Kris. We were meant to be.

Several movies later, Elise passed out on my bed. She was adamantly against caffeine consumption, and thus a heavy sleeper. My digital clock read *'8:00 pm'*. The sun had set and darkness shrouded over the sky. I picked out a dark black spandex mini dress, some tattered stockings, and boots to wear. I added dark red lipstick and black eyeshadow to my look and finished off with mesh arm warmers.

A painful wail came out with every inch I moved my bedroom window up. Still, I continued to open it, cringing with every noise, hoping neither Elise or my dad would wake up. When it finally opened all the way, I plunged through and instantly realized my wardrobe's limitations as I slithered out.

The crisp fall air hit my chest as I pulled myself into the dangerous world. My dress pulled my legs together, and I clambered out of the window instead of the graceful swoop I'd hoped for. My combat boots pounded the pavement when I landed. They kept me a step behind from where I would have been with good old sneakers. I spotted Kris's black car waiting for me around the corner as I reached the end of the street lined with identical suburban houses.

Kris smiled at me as I slid into the passenger seat. I had successfully made it without getting caught. He placed his hand on the stick shift, and the car drove down the empty streets.

"Where are we going?" That was the first thing I could say once I caught my breath.

He looked at me with his mysterious and playful smile. "It's a surprise."

"It always is with you!" I teased.

Kris drove through the streets like a bat out of hell to wherever he was taking me now.

Chapter Twenty
My Blood for You

We passed streets lined with desolate strip malls, grocery stores, and restaurants. All very familiar to me. The music coming from the car radio played an 80's dark wave song. The sound the music created gave ambiance to the moment. I viewed large ancient oak trees and towering colonial homes of the Garden District through my window.

I knew where Kris was taking me now. He was driving to the graveyard. My graveyard. The car slowed down as he approached the old wrought-iron gate. The main gate to the cemetery was locked. People became protective of the cemeteries since drunks or homeless people, or even people looking for a thrill, would damage the tombstones. I personally did not understand why anyone would want to defile such a beautiful place. Kris parked his car on the curb next to the entrance.

"I've got this; I know how to unlock the gate." I opened my car door confidently.

"I know, too." Kris's mouth bent slightly upwards as he stepped out of the car.

I watched him pull his hand through the gate and snap it open like I always did. A smile crossed my face as we drove through the lines of gravestones; each stone had its own unique design and fixture. He then reached the back of the graveyard to my favorite place. The place he met me just last night at the large stone gazebo.

Kris stopped his car right next to the palace of my dreams. I stepped out with a smile as he extended his arm toward the gazebo before us. A small circle of candles along the railing around the gazebo with candlelight flickered in the darkness. The shadows cast from the light were in sync with the fall breeze. A small white lace cloth was on the dusty floor with red rose petals scattered around. My mouth dropped open as excitement welled up within me. It was so beautiful.

"How did you know?' I questioned him.

"Know what?" he said coyly.

"That this is my favorite place." I walked towards the gazebo.

"I sensed it last night when I ran into you here. Based on your stack of books in the corner." He pointed to the rose terrace in my secret corner. I traced my fingers across the stone gazebo wall.

I shrugged. "I have spent many summers here, reading every vampire novel I could get my hands on."

"Come in with me." Kris led me into the gazebo as he held my hand in his.

I stood across from him on the lace cloth. The October air brushed against my chest and hung within my breath, sending a chill down my spine. Tall forest-like trees surrounded us in the gazebo, and the leaves on them whispered and rattled along with the air. Kris's eyes met mine; he had a serious look on his face. The candlelight danced around us. Why did he take me here? He leaned down on one knee. My knees shook, and I stepped back. He noticed my hesitation but continued.

"Dalia, you have captivated me." He looked up into my eyes longingly. "You are the object of my desire, Dalia, and if you accept me..." He paused as if to regroup his thoughts. "I would like to take your hand and initiate you to our clan. To lead with me as my queen."

What could I say? I had waited for something like this all my life. All the years I spent fawning after each vampire prince in every romance novel I read. Only in my wildest dreams did I imagine a dark, handsome vampire prince like Kris. He captivated my heart. Kris delicately opened a small black box with a silver chain necklace. An amulet hung perfectly on the chain. Silver covered the top of the amulet, with a glass vial filled with blood.

"My blood for you," Kris spoke with sincerity.

I picked up the amulet, studying every detail before looking back down at Kris. His face shone in the moonlight along with his crystal eyes.

I extended my hand to his. "I will."

"Then my immortal bride you will be." He stood up and swooped his arm around my shoulder.

I could swear a league of bats flew from the gazebo roof at that moment. Kris caressed my waist and moved his hands to trace my chest. His hand traveled up to clasp the amulet's chain around my neck. Passion filled his eyes. My hand trembled as I traced the vial below my neck.

My blood for you. His words sang through my soul as he kissed me beneath the moonlight.

Chapter
Twenty-One
The Queen

"Dalia, what is your desire for this marriage in the clan for us?" His question intrigued me. It sounded so beautiful when he formed the word. *Us.*

"What are yours?" I whispered. I felt the strength from his hand as it glided down my arm. I wanted to just surrender everything to him. He was my perfect gothic prince.

"In the clan, they expect that I will find a queen. A leader to take Zayn's place when we are ready. I see that in you. You are royalty."

My entire soul melted. I glanced at the lattice covered in long vines with roses behind us. It reminded me of a rose and how nothing lasts. Like my parents' marriage.

"Are you okay?" Kris asked, snapping me out of my thoughts. He held my hand close to his lips and kissed me tenderly on my wrist. Maybe he had sensed my doubts?

"As my eternal bride, would you let me drink from you?" he added.

My harrowing moment with Valentin flashed before my eyes. Valentin made my bones shudder. The night of the concert was traumatic and magical at the same time.

"Would you be willing to give your blood to the clan?" Kris continued. "It doesn't happen often, but we pull together to supply for the clan's needs."

I nodded silently; I didn't see any harm in sharing my blood. I cut myself enough to know that I didn't care for it much. Kris would surely enjoy the addiction I had. And if this was the way to become his queen...

"Dalia." Kris pulled me out of my thoughts. "If you are sure you want to be part of the clan, the vow cannot be broken. Please understand that. There are eternal consequences if not."

I looked out among the gravestones. Eternal consequences? Like hell? I didn't believe in hell anyway.

"Would I be damned to hell for eternity?" I joked in response.

Kris stood up from the gazebo floor and brushed off his black jeans. "We already are, dear. This world wasn't made for us." He laughed until a flashing light behind the gazebo stopped us both.

"It's the graveyard keeper! Let's go!" Kris exclaimed.

We both ran away like two little kids who got caught toilet papering on Halloween. We left behind the candles, lace cloth, and everything in the gazebo as we sprinted for the gates. Kris was exasperated as soon as we got inside the car. Laughter kept me from breathing as I buckled my seat belt.

"That was an adventure," Kris chuckled again.

He skidded around the corner and out of the graveyard. My body settled into the car seat as I held on tight to the door handle and he whisked us away.

A sense of victory flowed through me as we approached the Bat-cave. I traced the small blood-red amulet with my hand. This was the love that I had always dreamed of. The moonlight shone brighter than before. Everything felt so surreal. It could've been the adrenaline pumping through my body after running away from the graveyard or that I had just been proposed to.

"Let's go inside." Kris's long trench coat swayed as he stepped out of the car.

The Elvira 2.0 lady was safely guarding the door, decked out as usual. This time, with Kris holding my hand, I walked by confidently. She didn't even think to stop me like before. Smoke entered my lungs as we walked through the dance floor. The air of the club had the usual sense of darkness. One that I had become familiar with. Kris opened the door to the secret red hallway, and I walked inside. This place was now a part of me. I was going to be the queen. Valentin and another clan member that I did not recognize slipped out of the gathering room. They both gave me a smirk. I knew that Valentin didn't like me being with Kris. Maybe he heard about the recent development in our relationship?

"What are you up to, boys?" I jeered back at them.

Kris smiled at me, surprised by my sense of authority. They both looked to be in shock as I referred to them as *boys*. I knew that my smile, and my mannerisms, told them I was better than them now. Valentin shook his head at me. The other clan member merely shrugged his shoulders as they walked away to the door leading out to the dance floor. The pounding music and the fog of the club spilled into the hallway as they did. What if he already knew what was happening? The palms of my hands began to sweat as I clenched them. Instead of confidence, all that was left within me was fear of Valentin and what he could do to me as I walked through Kris' bedroom door.

"They have no idea about who you are going to become." Kris motioned for me to come in.

The room was dimly lit, smelling heavy of incense and cigarette smoke. Only a small sliver of moonlight shone through the basement window and illuminated the coffin in the corner of his bedroom. This time, it was laid open on the stone floor. I inched towards the coffin. It was a dark brown color with deep red satin on the inside. Did they take this from a real funeral home? Looking at the coffin made me lose any confidence about Kris or the clan. Despite any power I could attain within the clan, or even the love I found with Kris. Perhaps Elise was right in her sense of caution. What exactly did the clan get into?

"Kris," I called him from the other side of the room. "Just curious, does the clan do anything concerning this coffin?"

He grinned with a sense that he was pleased that I had asked him.

"When you are initiated into the clan, you spend one night in the coffin. It's not necessary, just a tradition and representation of what we believe," he explained.

"How does it reflect what you believe?" My naivety reflected in my voice.

"We sleep in a coffin to represent our death as a mortal and our resurrection as an immortal. We believe that three days after death, we are going to resurrect into an eternal being. That's why we are not vampires... yet." Kris touched the coffin along with me.

The wood was smooth. The details on the top of the coffin formed the symbol of a cross. There it was again, a crucifix. What significance did the cross have with a vampire clan?

"What about the cross?" I continued asking questions to pull myself back into the conversation with Kris, pointing to the engravement.

125

"Remember when I said my grandparents were Roman Catholic?"

I nodded. "Yes, I do."

"They believe a lot of the same things, too." He paused. "My parents just took a different aspect of it."

"I thought vampires were repelled by the cross," I replied. I didn't know anything about Catholicism. I only knew about the tall ivory figurines of Jesus, a man dying on a cross, or pictures of nuns with rosaries praying next to a stained-glass window in relation to it.

"Dalia, we believe there is a significance in self sacrifice. Life is in the blood. There is no denying that," Kris corrected.

"So, you take it from the bible?"

"Not the bible, but rather, from reality." Kris gently caressed my shoulders, and I sensed that he was eager for more than just a simple conversation.

His eyes set on mine as his fangs peeked from his lips. Kris leaned in. His breath hit my neck, and his lips followed. I closed my eyes. I could feel my knees weaken as his body pressed against mine. He kissed my neck until he reached my mouth. His fangs gently pressed into my lips. I felt like I couldn't breathe, and all my blood rushed to my head as he kissed me. My heart stopped as he gently caressed my hair. My arms glided across his back, as his hands did mine. After a couple minutes, we both stared into each other's eyes. Our hearts and breaths matched each other's in this moment, in sync. We chased each other in our oblivion.

Kris reached for a lighter and flicked it to light the candle on the table. Then he picked up a small blade that was on the table next to the coffin and sat next to the table. His hand raised the blade to the fire.

"Your wrist?" He looked down at my already carved-up arm covered by my long-sleeve shirt.

I extended my hand to him. He pulled up my sleeve and examined the many scars, his gaze loving and delicate. Did he want to drink blood from me?

"Your scars can have a purpose now. Your blood is worth so much more than self-hatred." He placed his lips on my most recent wound, from the graveyard. Then he continued gently kissing each scar. The warmth of every kiss creating a surge of love.

A tear traveled down my cheek. I had never felt such kindness. His eyes searched my arm, studying each scar. He placed the blade on my arm and looked up at me.

"Are you okay if I drink from you?"

I nodded. Blood slithered out from my arm as he etched the blade into my skin. He wrapped his mouth around my wrist with passion. I gasped at first and pulled my arm away.

"Are you okay?" He paused. Small red streaks of my blood stained the corners of his mouth.

"Yes." My mouth twitched a bit as I uttered the words, confirming that he could drink from me. "Yes, I am."

Kris leaned forward and continued to drink. I felt his teeth slightly pulling across my skin and his breath across my forearm as he drank deeply. I turned toward the coffin, and a sudden shiver went down my spine.

Kris stopped suddenly to peer up at me. His eyes looked different. They were the same eyes, but now they had a glimmer of hatred within them. It was like they had turned into pools of darkness.

Kris stared at me as he noticed the fear on my face. "What is it?"

I sat back in fear. "I..." I didn't have the words as I looked down at my bloodied wrist.

"This is our life together, Dalia." He brushed my hair back and then pulled his lips to my arm. He kissed the wound, still bleeding. "There is redemption for every drop of blood."

He stepped back and stood by the window. His eyes gleamed with shadows. A pale face surrounded by long, dark hair. Sharp fangs covered in my blood peeked from his lips. He was the vampire lover I dreamed of. Or so I thought. Why didn't it feel like I'd always imagined? My eyes burned as I tried hard to fight back the tears. I couldn't cry now. I covered my face with my hands to hide the few tears that escaped my eyes. Kris turned and brushed the back of his hand across my cheek.

"My Dalia, don't be afraid. I am here with you, only to protect you."

I lowered my hands from my face to look back at him. I didn't know what to expect after what just happened. Why did I feel afraid?

"Let me take you home. This must be too much at once. You need to rest," he said softly.

I stood up and covered up my new wound with my shirt sleeve. Kris took my hand as we walked out the bedroom door. I turned back to catch a glimpse of the moonlight shining on the coffin once more. Why was this different than simply cutting myself? Kris took from me, he took my blood. It wasn't just me taking from myself. It was a spiritual transaction. One that would shift the very fabric of who I was.

Chapter
Twenty-Two
The Amulet

KRIS DROPPED ME OFF a couple of yards away from my house and watched me as I walked down the secluded street. Not getting any panicked calls or texts from my dad or Elise was a good sign. He didn't even notice I left.

Stepping inside the house, I escaped the chilly fall air and embraced the sanctity of my room. A sigh of relief hit my body as I collapsed down to the floor next to my window. I had made it back. My alarm clock read 3 a.m. I touched the blood amulet nestled between my chest. Kris loved me. He loved me.

Swallowing, I set my head down on my pillow as I laid down on the comforter sheet on my bed. Elise was still passed out on one side, sleeping as hard as a rock. I held the amulet in my hand, tracing it softly, until the comfort of my bed and the blankets surrounding my body caused me to drift into a slumber of my own.

I felt a heavy breath upon my neck and an unusual presence behind me. Valentin? I turned to see a figure I had not seen before. It wasn't Valentin or even Kris this time. A knight dressed in black armor stood before me. Darkness covered his face. I moved back and bumped into something behind me. I wanted to keep a safe distance from this stranger. His very presence disturbed me.

I felt my hand land on something smooth. I turned to see my hand on a dark wooden coffin. It had a silver cross inlaid upon it, like the one in Kris's room. I placed my hand on the cross, and electricity ran through me. My body froze as a sense of death itself struck me. I struggled to breathe in. The stark contrast between the life that pumped through my veins and what ran through my body through this cross. Death itself.

"Will you die with me?" a harrowing voice spoke through the darkness covering the knight's face. The same chill I felt with Kris ran through my body. I pondered his words as I laid my hand still upon the pewter cross.

"You will be given a new life. You will never die," he whispered.

The little amount of breath left within my lungs was taken. I reached for the coffin to keep my balance and looked up at the knight. Small flames of fire appeared from the darkness on his face. He moved closer to me. Those were his eyes? The fire pierced down into the depths of my soul as he spoke to me.

"I spilled my blood for you." The knight pointed to my heart.

I looked down to see a small ruby necklace around my neck in the shape of a heart. It was empty, unlike the amulet from Kris. Crimson red blood began to fill the empty glass pendant. Sweat dripped down my forehead, and I closed my eyes. *I'm not here. I can't be*. Relief flooded my body. My hand glided across the soft tufts on my comforter. My eyes opened to the darkness of my bedroom. Kris had shown me the coffin in his room. That was real, but what just happened? It was just a dream. I was not really there, I was *here*.

I unwound the cold chain that sat across my neck and placed the amulet on my nightstand. Maybe I should take this off for now. Whatever my dream meant, it had something to do with the necklace. I pulled my black down comforter around my shoulders. Pulling the serenity of home back into my mind as well. This was the first nightmare I'd had in ages. Did Kris have any connection to the dream? The blue nightlight on my nightstand gave me security that nothing or no one was lurking in my room at least. I breathed in the stillness of my darkened room and closed my eyes to sleep.

Chapter
Twenty-Three

Fangs

A PUNGENT SMELL HIT my face. The morning met me sooner than I had wished as Elise waved a hemp protein breakfast bar close to my nose.

"Good morning!" she exclaimed right as my first eyelid cracked open. I jolted and then sighed as I realized it was her. It was just her.

"My trick never fails!" A sense of victory covered her face.

"Elise! Can you not do that?" I covered my nose with a groan.

"What is this?" Her eyes wandered over to my nightstand.

Her two pale bony fingers held up my amulet necklace, the chain pinched cautiously between the one half of her hand. She cringed.

"Is that real blood?" she questioned me and looked closer. "It's beautiful!"

"Yes." I quickly snatched it from her. "It's just a gift Kris gave me the other day."

"Weird, but okay." She shrugged in response and packed up her cloth tie-dyed bag. "I'm gonna head home now. My mom probably will wonder where I'm at anyway."

"Okay, I'll see you when you pick me up for rehab tomorrow?" I checked with her that we were for sure back to normal.

"Yep." She pulled her fist towards me to pound it and left my bedroom.

Her house was only around the corner from mine. I heard the sputter of the old bug start up and drive away. Normally, she would walk to save the environment from air emissions for such a short distance. Her absence left me in the silence of my room again. I started to text Kris, but then I stopped. I really didn't understand what my dream last night was about, but the knight reminded me of Kris. He had this... sense of authority. Suddenly, my phone vibrated, and a message popped up. It was Kris.

"Batcave tonight?" It read.

I *could* go to the Batcave tonight. My dream could have been my brain processing my emotions from yesterday. It was remarkable. Never in my wildest imagination could I have found myself with someone as perfect as Kris. Every time we kissed, I felt like I was in heaven. His eyes and his words soothed my aching soul. Though the clan made me feel uncomfortable sometimes, I was allured by the mystery of it all.

Kris drinking my blood last night I was sure would be the first of many experiences. Kris seemed to savor drinking from me. It didn't feel like what I expected, or even as sensational as what I had read in many of my vampire novels. From what I had read, the vampire couldn't resist even the scent of blood. Kris did act differently when he was drinking from me. It was as if something possessed him. He was tender with me.

"Yes, pick me up?" I replied to Kris.

"7 p.m., my queen." He texted back.

I put on a deep red shirt with an overlaying black corset, a black pleated skirt, torn up leggings, and my combat boots. My natural color disappeared as I brushed my whitest goth foundation across my cheekbones. A deep red lipstick over a black color finished it all off. Still, something shone through despite the amount of dark eyeshadow and lipstick I put on. I could not hide the glow of a girl in love. I picked up the amulet from my night nightstand. My fingers shook as I held the blood vial in between them. I placed the amulet around my neck. I must wear it for Kris if anything else. The love I felt from Kris when I wore it radiated past the fear from my dream.

"Where are you going looking like that?"

I barely stepped out of my bedroom door before my dad was already breathing down my neck.

"I always look like this." I shrugged my shoulders and casually walked down the hall towards the front door.

"Well, where are you going?" He pushed harder.

I tried not to sound defensive. "I'm going to hang out with Kris."

He looked at me as if it confused him that I wasn't hanging out with Elise.

"It's fine, Dad." I insisted.

He shook his head a bit and turned to walk towards his room. "Fine."

I turned around and rolled my eyes. Don't see, don't tell. That was my dad's rule, I guess. It kept us both sane. White lights shone through the dining room window. He's here!

"Bye, Dad!" I yelled as I ran out the front door.

A sleek black Mercedes sat in the driveway. Kris stood there with a bouquet of roses in his hands. His attire was grungy with a bit of class, dressed up in a black button-down shirt with long sleeves, along with black jeans and combat boots. His hair was swooped to one side. I loved it. He extended the bouquet out to me. Expressions or answers left my mind as blood rushed to my face. He placed the bouquet into my quivering hand, then opened the passenger door for me.

"Is there some kind of inheritance in the family?" I asked as I traced my hands across the black leather interior.

"We do get a lot of profit from the club. This is my Uncle's car." Kris glared at me just as much as my dad, as I sat into the leather passenger seat. "And you are beautiful as always."

He leaned towards me, picked up my hand, and gently kissed it. My heart melted as it always did in these moments. I looked up towards the moon. It was a beautiful quarter shape, promising it would become fuller soon.

"The moon." I paused as I stared at the ethereal sky. Kris reflected the same admiration as I did.

He turned back to me. "You are much more beautiful, Dalia."

I looked down at my boots. I didn't know how to handle his compliments. It was still strange for me to receive compliments from a guy, let alone one as perfect as he was.

"I wanted to take you to the Batcave again tonight. There is more you need to know about the clan." he continued.

I sat in the passenger seat, still gazing up through the sunroof as Kris drove. I admired the stars that dared to shine past the city lights. Every moment I breathed in felt like a fantasy. The stars above only reminded me that what I was living was real. The car eventually rolled to a stop before the Batcave. My eyes turned to Kris, finding he looked stoic, with the moonlight beaming on his face. A knock on the window made us jump. Zayn smiled through it, and I pushed the door open.

"Alicia is at the front, right? Why are you up here?" Kris inquired of her. "Or are you waiting for us?" he asked before she could reply.

She took my hand with her eloquent long black fingernails.

"I'm waiting for her, your beautiful bride." Zayn kissed my cheek. She gave me the warmth of a mother. This must be why Kris loves her so much. "I have something to show you." She gleamed with the biggest smile I had ever seen her with.

With that, she pulled me inside the club. The booming music, dancing clubgoers, and all the excitement inside didn't faze me anymore. This had become my home.

"I guess I'll wait here for you." Kris walked towards the booths next to the bar and picked up a red wine glass.

"Wait." I reached my hand out to him. I didn't want him to leave me alone.

But he didn't hear me past the loud music. The bartender had already started to ask him for a drink. What choice did I have now? I followed Zayn to the black secret door. She led me down the blood-red hallway and to a door I had not been inside before. Maybe it was her bedroom? She jangled the knob a bit before pulling it open.

"Don't mind the door. It gets stuck with these old walls." She smiled at me.

I stepped inside a dark room after her. The floor, walls, and even ceiling were painted black. My eyes searched across the space. There was a sewing machine with various material scraps around it. Large reams of fabric were lined across the wall, and sewing materials were strewn across shelves. But the desk in the corner looked different. It appeared to have medical devices. Blood vials, needles, and a small silver glass with another wine cellar rack. Was this where they extracted blood from donors? The moonlight beaming from another small window like Kris's room shone into the corner of the space. The light revealed the most beautiful thing. Zayn walked to the corner with me.

"It's..." I was at a loss for words. *So beautiful*, I thought as I pointed to the black corseted bodice.

"Would you like to try on your dress?" She turned to me. Her eyes seemed pleased that she could give it to me.

"For me?" I gasped, staring at her with my mouth agape.

Zayn nodded as I gawked at the beautiful dress. "It was my dress when I got initiated into the clan." She patted the corset with admiration. "I've added some stuff to it to suit your style, though."

"This must be nostalgic for you!" I replied.

My eyes passionately scanned over the garment. It was ankle-length with black lace, sequined with black beads throughout the dress. A line of dark blood-red gemstones accentuated the plunging neckline.

"Well, do you want to try it on?" Zayn stopped my admiration.

"Of course!" I stood back as she grasped the garment from the mannequin.

The dress fit snugly across my shoulders, and enhanced my waistline, falling to my ankles as expected. It contrasted well with my pale complexion. With the moonlight billowing through the window and onto the mirror before me, I looked like the vampire goddess I always imagined. Nothing could have been more perfect. I touched the small gemstones lining my decolletage. My amulet was set between my collarbones. The dress perfectly framed my chest. The deep crimson color of the gemstones reminded me of something. They were cool to the touch. My dream with the knight? I stood for a second gazing as the dress beamed in the moonlight.

"May I?" Zayn pulled me out of my thoughts and began to tighten my corset strings.

I gasped for air as she cinched my waistline in. The figure I desired was soon reflected in the oblong mirror before me. My chest heaved for a breath as Zayn laced and tied the last bow on the back. She then turned for a moment and set two earrings next to each side of my face.

"For the night of the ceremony." She placed them close to each ear and then placed them in my hand. They matched the red gemstones on my neckline. "Now, how would you like your hair for the night of the ceremony?"

Zayn gently traced my dark black hair. Soft waves trailed on the outer edges of my shoulders. My usual box hair color dyed it so black it enmeshed with the color of the dress.

"I would suggest you have your hair up for logistical reasons." She gently touched my neck.

"Logistical?" I looked back into the mirror and tried to imagine what I might look like on the night of the ceremony. My hair could be curled up like that of a maiden in a period drama.

"When Kris drinks from you, my love," Zayn replied simply.

"I think I might want some of it down on the night of the ceremony, but some of it pinned up too." I loved having my hair down. It looked perfect with the dress.

"We can work with that." She touched my shoulder, giving way to the waves upon them. "You will be the most perfect queen for Kris."

I looked into the mirror once more. Never could I have imagined that I might be so beautiful. Zayn played with my hair, twisting it into a long braid. Her touch was as soothing as my mother's when she used to braid my hair as a child. She left the lower half of my hair to flow past my shoulders and pulled the rest back into the braid.

"Dalia." Zayn looked at me with intent. I had fallen into a comforting stillness as she braided my hair. Her voice pulled me out of my own rested gaze. "I also wanted to tell you details about the initiation ceremony."

"Okay," I replied. My eyes directed towards her as she spoke.

"It will happen on All Hallow's Eve."

"All Hallow's Eve?" A light rapping on the door interrupted my shock.

"We will be out in a second!" Zayn yelled towards the door. "You can't see your bride in her dress until the ceremony." She chuckled. "He still isn't used to waiting."

I still was in a slight state of shock about her comment. Zayn's fingers moved quickly to unlace my corset. She had done this before. I stepped out of the long dress and put my clothes on. He pounded on the door once more, even though only a few minutes had passed.

"I'm almost done," I called out to him.

I pulled on my spandex dress and then picked up my belt that overlaid my skirt. The belt would have to wait. I slipped my feet into my combat boots, without even tying the laces, and walked over to open the door with my hair disheveled from putting my clothes back on.

"You're so eager to see me, Kris," I teased.

Kris walked in with a confident smile. I started to put my studded belt on as he walked past me into the room. Valentin stood by the door and rolled his eyes.

"I don't want to know." he sighed and looked down at me as I put on my belt.

"If only you could." Kris chimed back. I slapped him on the shoulder as we both laughed.

"It's not what he thinks," I added in, trying to clear the air. Valentin had already walked out into the club before we noticed he was gone.

"Let's go to the clan meeting room." Kris held my hand and led me further down the hallway, to the last black door. Back in the clan's meeting room, he guided me to his signature booth.

"So, Zayn told me my initiation is on All Hallow's Eve. That's..." I gave him a serious stare and sat down on the red pleather booth right next to him. He didn't look surprised. Beautiful and romantic as that sounded, Hallow's Eve was just this Friday.

"It's okay if you don't want to." He looked a little disappointed and grabbed my hand tenderly. "I understand."

"No!" I interrupted him, growing flustered. The words fell from my lips. "I mean, no, I want to do it," I stumbled into agreement with his desire. "My favorite holiday is Halloween, but I didn't expect my initiation to happen so soon."

Maybe I should consider myself lucky that he would be so committed to me or even that Kris desired me to be his queen in the clan. He sat there with loving eyes as he took me in.

"I would love to," I replied calmly and with confidence back at Kris.

I leaned my head on his shoulder. He would be my vampire knight for sure.

"It's so sweet seeing Kris in love." Zayn approached the table and sat next to me. "But the truth is this..." She pierced her jade-green eyes over at me sharply. "Kris needs a bride to be with him as he takes over the vampire clan."

I hesitated to respond as all my insecurities about myself rose. Did this mean that Kris really loved me, or that he was just looking for someone to fill a role? Kris squeezed my hand in his. The warmth of his hand filled mine as he winced at Zayn.

"Dalia, I want you to be by my side because I love you. This isn't just anything. This is an eternal agreement between us." he assured me.

Inside, I felt a sudden weight of what that meant. The heaviness of it.

"You will be my perfect queen." He placed his hand on my cheek, slowly down to my neck, and then to the amulet below it.

I became breathless as his fingers caressed the amulet. I was going to be joined with Kris and be his queen. Anticipation welled up in my chest. His eyes squinted as he smiled at me.

"I have something else for you. To make it official." He pulled out a small coffin-shaped box from his pocket. Then he used his other hand to open the box. Two perfectly sharpened fangs sat inside surrounded by black velvet.

"It's an early gift for the ceremony." He smiled, showing his own fangs. Zayn suddenly looked at him with a sense of caution. "Alex said it was okay," he replied to her stare. "You're part of the clan, and you're my bride, Dalia," he whispered in my ear. "Let me put them on for you."

I cautiously opened my mouth as he stuck each fang onto my top two incisors.

"There you go." He pressed the second fang onto my tooth, firmly nudging it up.

I pulled out my phone and turned my camera on to see what I looked like. My smile was no longer mine. I gazed at the fangs, but I didn't see myself. I saw who I was *now*. This was who I always wanted to be. Kris leaned in to kiss my forehead as I smiled at the camera.

"They're perfect." I beamed back at Kris.

"Just like you are perfect," he remarked.

Chapter
Twenty-Four
Dreadful

THE MIRROR BEFORE ME reflected a cold, blank stare. I did not know what lay before me tonight, but I was ready. The corset-cinched dress clasped my body in. Red lipstick framed my lips, while black hair flowed past my chest. The contrast of pale against dark reflected my heart at this moment. Pulled between the serenity of this moment yet still disturbed by the chaos roaring inside of me. Was I making the right decision?

I turned towards the window facing a nearby flower garden and breathed in to get my last breath of fresh air. The thorns from the bouquet of roses held tight between my black gloves reminded me that I was there. I traced the small ruby-red necklace around my neck. My brows furrowed. It was empty. Confused, I traced it with my thumb lightly. A faint echoing of an organ playing down the dressing room corridor stirred me, and my eyes snapped up towards the hall. I ran across the cobblestone and flung open the wooden door. *Wait...* I gazed at my trembling hand.

My feet moved despite my mind saying to stop. I was to be joined with another soul for eternity. The cascading staircase led me to a brick corridor just beyond a set of tall wooden doors. Anticipation swelled up within me as the organ player struck the last note. The song resounded throughout the sanctuary as the doors began to divide. A small crack of light chased away the darkness that surrounded me. Its luminance proved blinding with every inch of my red dress slowly revealed as the light cascaded up until it reached the crown of my head.

I looked up at the altar with the countenance of a beaming bride. My eyes fluttered like my heart until my groom turned. I opened my eyes, anticipating Kris, donned in all black, standing at the altar. No, not Kris, but the knight. His voice exuded from the darkness of his face.

"Will you be my bride?"

I looked down at him, his knee bent. A black silver-lined coffin was laid halfway open next to him as the knight stretched his hand towards it.

"Come and die with me. Be my bride, and we will live for an eternity." The shadows of his face were illuminated yet again with the fire of his eyes.

I dared not to turn away, though my breath became heavy. I must not look away. I trembled in fear at the knight. He stood back up boldly. With no reservations, he looked at me with absolute possessiveness. His stare caused me to cower, and I looked down to my knees next to an altar covered in a black cloth. The knight placed a silver goblet in my hand. This was not Kris. Why did it feel like it? I swirled the unknown concoction in the goblet. Was this blood? I shuddered and at the same moment, the smell of flames filled my nostrils, and my arm felt the warmth of fire.

The coffin before us burst into flames, and my heart raced in my chest.

"Drink of my blood. Eternal life, my love." He raised the goblet up to my lips.

A numbness immediately hit my lips as my mouth filled with the liquid inside. I felt a pure joy fill my spirit as I drank the blood. But a wretched pounding in my head stopped me. My hands became heavy as I looked down at the heart-shaped amulet. Blood began to fill it. A pounding caused me to shudder again, but not within my head. Sweat trickled down my forehead, and the pounding only grew. *I'm here.* The tuft cushions around me jolted me awake, and I sat up in bed. My door shook, and the sound of my dad knocking behind it echoed through the room.

"Dalia!" my dad's voice resounded in the hallway.

"What?" I shot back, resting my hand on my forehead. Last night was just too late.

I fell back on my mattress, still dressed in my dress. Getting up, I looked in my vanity mirror and at the black makeup that lined my eyes like a raccoon. I could at least just wash my face before I go, right? I walked across to the hallway and into the bathroom. But my dad stopped me as soon as he stepped inside and shut the bathroom door.

"Late night?" he pressed.

I think he wanted to believe that I was up late, reading a book like I normally did. He stepped closer and smelled my hair.

"You smell like smoke," he said flatly.

Crap! I forgot. The Batcave always had the hollow fog of smoke hanging around. It wasn't a luminous effect from the fog machines on the Batcave as much as it was just the smokers who frequented the club.

"I got a call from Mrs. Gracie. Did you go to treatment on Friday?" His eyebrow raised. "Make sure you make it there today, Dalia."

"Okay, Dad," I grunted and closed the bathroom door, breathing a sigh of relief when his footsteps faded down the hallway.

The water from the sink cooled my face, and I sprayed my clothes with perfume. This would have to do for today. I quickly re-lined my eyes with eyeliner. Looking into my own green eyes reminded me of Zayn. I only hoped that one day, I could be like her. She always looked like she walked straight out of a Gothic Beauty Magazine.

"Bye, Dad!" I called out, pouring a small cup of coffee and taking a gulp of it. Coffee was like my salvation for a day like this that could drag on forever. Elise was sitting quietly inside the Bug, chomping on her hemp bar for breakfast when I opened the passenger door and slid inside.

"Want one?" she offered me. I cringed and shook my head. Those bars tasted like tree bark to me.

"No, thanks."

"Are you doing, okay? You seem kind of out of it." She leaned into my shoulder and sniffed me. "And you smell like smoke."

"I know, I know." I put my head against the window and sighed. Elise always had a way of stating the obvious. Yet she seemed to carry an innocent tone in each of her questions. "I was out late with Kris last night," I explained.

She tilted her head. Her go-to expression when she was confused.

"Out late doing what?" she prodded with a knowing smile.

"Trust me, it's not what you think." I laughed lightly. "Elise, I didn't tell you everything Saturday because I didn't know how to explain it yet." I pulled the amulet chain out of my shirt. I felt almost a sense of Deja-vu from my dream. The vial was full of blood. "This is more than just any amulet. Inside is Kris's blood. It's a proposal. At least, for the vampire clan it is."

Her hand tapped uneasily on the top of the steering wheel. "What? Dalia, that's so..." Her mouth gaped open, as she was at a loss for words.

"But you can't tell anyone!" I insisted.

"Don't you think it's kind of soon? Like, what do you mean by a proposal? A marriage proposal?" she questioned. I could tell she was trying to be sensitive towards my feelings. But she pulled a face at her last word.

"Kind of," I reassured her with my hand on her shoulder. "And it's like a marriage proposal but into the clan. I will be part of the clan."

Elise took a deep breath and backed up from the driveway.

Finally, she said, "I trust you, Dalia." She placed her hand firmly onto mine.

There was silence throughout the entire ten-minute drive to Sweetwater. I just hoped I didn't offend her; she was my best friend. But if she was my best friend, she should offer nothing but support for me. In the silence, I wondered about everything that Zayn and Kris explained to me last night. How the ceremony would go, what I would wear, and the fact that it would happen on All Hallow's Eve.

That would be a whole other thing to tell Elise. We always spent Halloween together. Just thinking about telling her made my palms begin to sweat. Then the dream from last night ran through my mind again. How could I have such a surreal dream too? It felt like my dreams synchronized with what was happening to me with the clan. Maybe I was stressing myself out about this too much, and it was manifesting in my sleep. Was I ready to commit to the clan?

Elise pounded on the brakes once she found a parking spot. The jolt pulled me from my thoughts. Kris quickly pulled up with his charger in the parking spot right next to us.

"I see one vampire who woke up early this morning." Elise teased. Kris smirked as he pulled his Ray-ban sunglasses off. He looked so polished as always.

"Late nights don't seem to bother him," I stated with a shrug. Could it be the extra iron he got from drinking blood on the regular? Or did he have supernatural powers since being initi-ated into the clan? Regardless of the hundreds of times I pulled an all-nighter to read a gripping thriller novel, I would have to adjust my body to stay up for the clan.

"Come on, Dalia." Elise rolled her eyes. This wasn't like her usual self. Her normal welcoming attitude faded.

"Elise." I placed my hand on her shoulder, frowning slightly.

Her small frame jolted with my hand on her shoulder. She spun to look at me. "What, Dalia?"

"What's wrong with you? Can we talk?"

"You want to talk *now*?" With that, she burst into tears. Her face turned red as she cried. "It's you and him!" She pointed toward Kris as he walked inside the building's dark glass doors. "You're slipping away and growing distant towards me. All be-cause of him." Her cheeks were red and nostrils wide as she breathed heavy with tears flowing from her eyes.

She huffed. "And there are things you aren't willing to talk to me about anymore. I can tell, but I don't know why. Why didn't you say anything about the amulet before today?"

"There are things I... just *can't* tell you. It's part of the clan rules, Elise." I sputtered back to her.

"That's crap! What happened to our friendship? We used to tell each other everything." She threw up her hands in exaspera-tion.

I sat silent. Tears leaked from my eyes and down my cheeks. I couldn't argue with her. She was right. Was this the price I would have to pay to be part of the clan? To be with Kris?

"Dalia!" Willa's voice broke the moment. I turned to see Willa's head pop out of the black entrance door. "The day is starting. Let's go!"

I began to tremble. I couldn't leave Elise. But hell, I also couldn't even look at her. Sullenly, I got out of the car and walked toward Sweetwater's doors.

"You need to come in here first thing." Willa led me down the hall to check into her office.

She pointed to the chair next to the blood pressure machine. Her hands began to roll up the long black sleeve on my arm, and my blood ran cold. *The cut!* Suddenly, reality began to sink in like Kris's teeth did on my arm. She rolled up the one without the cut. The blood pressure cuff tightened across it and then decompressed, but meanwhile, my heart was pounding like a drum.

"Your pressure is a bit high. Are you okay?" Willa looked straight at me.

"Yeah." I stared down at the floor, avoiding her piercing gaze.

She paused for a moment before saying, "We called your father about Friday."

"I know."

"Let me check your arms real quick."

Here it was, the breaking moment. She rolled up my sleeves on both of my arms. The gaping wound from Kris was revealed with the fresh blood-red color against the bright overhead office lights.

Willa nodded with a sigh. "You can talk to Gracie."

My heart banged within my chest again, and sweat beaded along my neck. Mrs. Gracie turned her head into the door from the hall.

"I thought I heard my name." She smiled at me, but her smile vanished as her eyes trailed down to the gash on my arm. "Come with me to my office," she said quietly.

Willa whispered into Mrs. Gracie's ear as we walked down the hall to the office. I glanced into the community room where Kris sat still in his desk. I was taking this hit for him. My heart pounded. Is he worth it?

"You broke our promise, Dalia." Mrs. Gracie had the same demeanor as always. Her eyes looked at me so innocently.

148

I just stared back at her. "What promise?"

"To not cut until we saw each other again."

I crossed my arms across my chest and leaned each elbow against the plush armchairs. What did she expect from me really? I didn't want or choose to be here. I didn't want to get 'better'.

"I'm going to have to call your father again." Mrs. Gracie leaned back in her seat. No need to let her know that a call to my dad wasn't an effective way of help or even discipline. "Until then..." She tilted her head. "Is there anything you need to talk about?"

Talk about? Anything? There was a lot. The fact that my mom left and never returned. The fact that I was losing my best friend because I loved a guy from rehab. I finally felt accepted into the clan yet now I was losing Elise because of it. For a second, my eyes trailed to Gracie and then back to the floor. What type of help could she be to me? Even if I trusted her, could she handle everything I went through the last few weeks? Or even the reason why I had a cut on my arm?

"No." I finally shook my head.

Gracie pointed at the door for me to go. I left and walked into the community room. Kris gave me an awkward smile as I sat in the back empty desk. He probably sensed that something was wrong. My watch buzzed a moment later.

"Are you okay?" A text from Kris illuminated the screen.

I turned to smile at him, to assure him I was fine. What's the worst that they could do, besides send me back to the hospital for lockdown? Well... anxiety rose in my chest, and I stared down at my desk. Yeah. They could do that.

My watch buzzed again. *"Let's go to the graveyard later."*

I nodded towards him. He knew what made me happy. He was my knight in shining armor during this dreadful moment.

Chapter
Twenty-Five
Graveyard

GREEN, ORANGE, AND BROWN leaves painted the trees towards the end of October in Louisiana. Along with the leaves scattered across the graveyard, the humid air left the only other impression that fall had fully come. I breathed it in as Kris held my hand. We walked among the tombstones until we paused by the stone gazebo. My head rested contentedly on his shoulder. I felt the beating of his heart close to my ear and breathed in deeply. This place was my sanctuary. A place away from my life. In the past, I'd read books, written poetry, and sometimes... I paused and grabbed my cut-up arm, turning towards the gazebo.

"What's on your mind?" Kris turned his gaze towards my arm as well.

I perched my combat boot on the side of the railing of the gazebo and pulled myself up to sit. "I've spent an endless amount of summer nights reading and daydreaming in this gazebo. I read vampire novels mostly..."

"Really now?" Kris moved in between my legs swinging off the gazebo railing. His torso fit snugly between my knees as he smirked. "Did you ever dream of someone like me?"

I looked away from his pressing eyes and up toward the sky. I didn't want to show him how I was a lovey-dovey, eager teenage girl, that every moment spent here I was just dreaming of a guy like him. Though, I absolutely was. Instead, I pushed his shoulder, jabbing at him.

"Don't get ahead of yourself," I scolded.

He smiled and offered his hand to me; I dismounted the railing as lady-like as I could. He led me to the stone bench we had sat on before together, and I placed my head on his shoulder. His height was ideal for me. It allowed me to rest right in the crevice of his chest and shoulder. My breath slowed as my body relaxed on his. No longer was I the loner pining away at my endless romance novels. I was here, in my own story.

"I want to ask you this, Dalia." Kris glanced down at me. "Would you like to get initiated here?"

"I would love to!" I immediately picked up my head from his chest, adoring the idea. "What time are we going to the ceremony? Can Elise come to the ceremony? Or at least the afterparty?" I swiftly went from a place of serenity to a place of endless questions.

"You know what..." Kris scrunched his face in thought. "Let's go to the Batcave. We can figure it all out with Zayn. She knows more about the ceremony's details than I do."

He brushed his hand across the top of my forehead and down my face tenderly.

"Don't worry." He smiled, sensing my unease.

"I would like to do it at night. I've always wanted a graveyard wedding with candlelight," I added.

"That's the only way to do it," he replied with his fangs peeking from behind his smile. Every second with him seemed so surreal.

The sunshine faded as we let the minutes together fade to hours. Every second felt filled with emotion. It was like living in a never-ending gothic poem when I was with him. Kris eventually led me to his car and to the Batcave. The orange and red hues of the sky lulled into black with the darkness of night.

Chapter Twenty-Six

Hallow's Dream

"You look stunning as always," I said to Zayn as I sat down in the booth with her.

She looked down at her grey tattered dress, inlaid with a waist-cinching corset. Her lips were red. Her heart-shaped face was painted with dark makeup lining her eyes. She was exactly what I wanted to be as a clan leader. Vampire queen. Her arms wrapped over my shoulders as she squeezed me tight. Her presence invoked a sense of calm and admiration in me. The very comfort I felt before my mom left. The softness of her voice was like honey. She then sat and took a sip from a black mug holding coffee.

"I want to know more about the ceremony." Her height loomed over me as I sat in the tufted chair next to her.

Zayn looked up at me, away from her cup of dark brew. "I guess I'm done writing for now, and I can tell you what you will be doing Friday night."

She leaned against the wall and pulled a black journal down into the booth.

"It is on All Hallow's Eve, of course, and it will be a full moon that night. Which just confirms to me that you are the perfect one to become an heiress of the clan. Even the moon is confirming your initiation." Her face brightened along with the tone of her voice. I had never seen her stray from her calm, stoic demeanor until now. Warmth rushed to my cheeks as I turned to smile at Kris. He approached the booth with a silver chalice in his hand.

"We will go to the graveyard; Alex will take you," Zayn continued as she turned towards Kris to take the small silver goblet. "During the ceremony, you will have to drink Kris's blood from the silver chalice first." Her eyes trailed down to my throat. "Then Kris will drink from your neck."

I felt my muscles tighten. Was she thirsty for my blood as well?

"This is to signify the giving to one another as a sacrifice. Do you think you can handle it?" Zayn asked carefully.

My heart pounded. This all kind of seemed a little dangerous to me, but I nodded.

"I will come and escort you and Kris to his car after the ceremony. We don't want you to get too weak from the blood loss." A smile played on her lips.

My eyes widened. "Blood loss? How much will I lose?"

"Less than the five liters in your body," Kris replied with sarcasm while hovering next to me.

"And no one can come with you,' Zayn added, securing her hand on top of mine. Her eyes were set firm on me as if she was staring me down. The coldness of her hand contrasted against the heat of my own. My pulse picked up its pace with every second her eyes set on me.

"I'm sure it will be what I've always dreamed of," I replied and looked down at the silver chalice again to observe the intricate designs with small red rubies. What was the significance of the silver goblet?

Kris looked down at me as he stood next to me by the booth. My breath stopped. The dream I had with the knight had a silver chalice too. There had to be some connection between the clan and my dreams. Kris moved to hold the chalice in front of me. His dark eyes penetrated my soul. They became pools of black swirling before me. Summoning me to come closer.

"Drink, my bride," he spoke to me, and each word elicited a shiver down my spine.

Closing my eyes, I drank. It didn't have the same taste as the other times. The blood rolled through my lips and down my throat smoothly—sweeter than before. Electric sensations surged through my being, and my body felt stronger. Empowered. This was *changing* me. As the last drop touched my lips, I breathed in deeply and opened my eyes to Kris. Kris smiled at me as he held the chalice up to my lips. I couldn't give in to fear.

"Life is within the blood," Kris whispered down at me, gently pulling the chalice away. Instantly, a longing deep inside of me urged for more. Kris's eyes, like sacred pools, drew me into him, and a smile crossed his face.

Bliss covered my entire being as he kissed my lips. But a clang of the doorknob jiggling made me flinch and pull away from our kiss. Kris plunged towards the doorway. The doorknob jangled for a minute and then swung forward. Valentin, with fire in his eyes, stormed in. He seemed ready for the kill as Vivid trailed in behind him.

"What is this about?" Valentin interrogated Zayn as he stared at me, his gaze ice-cold.

Zayn smirked, her demeanor holding not a hint of fear or hesitation. "I'm assuming you've heard the good news?" she drawled.

"I came here to confirm that my dad didn't go crazy and let this happen," he replied, almost yelling now.

Vivid stood behind Valentin with as much fear in her eyes as mine.

"Kris and Dalia are going to lead the clan, starting All Hallow's Eve," Zayn retorted as a matter of fact.

"You can't be serious." His eyes zoned in on me.

I don't know if it was the blood I just drank or because Kris was beside me, but I wasn't going to let Valentin push me around like he did the night of the concert. I stood up to face him, narrowing my eyes.

"You're just mad because Kris is going to lead the clan and you aren't," I snapped.

Kris clenched my hand in his, signaling for me to be quiet. He might have known Valentin's violent potential more than I did. Vivid's face turned red. Her hand formed into a fist. Like a magnet, she gravitated towards me until Valentin pushed her to the side. She looked up at him, shocked he had done that to her.

He sneered. "Don't worry, Vivid, I'll handle this," he set her straight.

Valentin inched close to my face. But I didn't flinch. I wouldn't let myself be afraid. Kris stepped in front of me, shielding me with his body.

"Valentin, mind your own business. The date is set; you knew this was coming!" Kris yelled.

Valentin turned just as red as Vivid. This was his kryptonite. If he was allowed to rip Kris and me to shreds at this moment, he would have.

"Don't be so sure that the clan is here to fulfill your little vampire girl dreams." He grinned, flashing his fangs at me as he peeked behind Kris. With that, he grabbed Vivid's hand and walked out the door.

The air was just as tense as when he was here. Zayn and Kris were still silent. My face hardened, and I was frozen in place. What did he know of love? I knew that Kris loved me. My knuckles whitened as I clenched my fist. I would stop at nothing.

Chapter Twenty-Seven

Open Wounds

THE NEXT MORNING, I pulled open the Volkswagen's creaky door and slipped into the passenger seat with caution. I wasn't sure what to expect from Elise after yesterday. There was silence the entire ride until Elise started tearing up before I opened my door to leave.

"Dalia... I'm so sorry about yesterday. It's just—"

"No, no. Wait." I shook my head and wrapped my arms around her, holding her tight. I leaned back and looked into her blue, trusting eyes. "I'm so sorry I didn't tell you the truth about the amulet."

I looked down at her shaking hand. She always got jittery when it came to intense conversations.

"From now on. If you ask me about something, I will tell you the truth!" I promised.

My statement was bold since I knew I couldn't tell her about the initiation. My stomach turned as the words fell from my lips. I hated being like this. But it seemed this was the cost of being in the clan.

"I love Kris, but not only him," I added. "I love you, too."

Her arms grasped me again. This time, our hug was so tight, that it felt like we melted together as her tears streamed onto my shoulder, her sniffles echoing through the car.

"Do you want to go to the mall after treatment today?" I added softly as I stroked her back. Elise smiled at me as she wiped away the last of her tears.

"Maybe they have some cool Halloween stuff for sale," she beamed, as finding good deals always made her happy. Although I was hesitant about how I would tell Elise about my ceremony on All Hallow's Eve coming up this weekend. I also had a sense of excitement towards it, too. Soon, I would become Kris's bride and the queen of a vampire clan. I felt like fate had finally met me. I was walking into my destiny. I bumped into Kris as I exited the Volkswagen door. Yes, I had run into fate. He smiled at me with his signature sexy grin.

"Excited for Friday?" Kris whispered in my ear as he gently tucked my hair behind it.

I pulled myself up to his face and gave him a slight kiss, tugging on his shirt collar lightly. "See you tonight at the cave?"

"Yes, my queen," he replied with a playful bow, amused by my antics.

I ran into the center's front door and down the hallway to Willa's office before Kris could get there first. This time, I went into treatment with a smile on my face.

"Glad to see you here and doing good this morning." Willa turned my arms and placed the pressure cuff on me as we went through our usual routine.

I stared dazed at the carpet. This Friday. This Friday, I would finally escape this monotony. That fact alone made walking to the Pepto-Bismol-pink therapy room that much easier. It was like I was floating. Mrs. Gracie's voice was just as bubbly as before. Each teen speaking about their week seemed to go by faster. I didn't care about any of this. Soon, their eyes were turned on me. The skinny girl I saw last week smiled slightly in my direction.

"So, Dalia, how has your week been so far?" Mrs. Gracie asked.

"It's been great," I replied with a genuine smile.

"Anything you want to share today?"

My skin buzzed. For a second, I swallowed deeply. Did she know? Maybe I was too bold with Kris in front of the center. Did she see us?

"No, not really." I stared back down at the floor tile. I didn't dare look back up at Gracie or make eye contact after that.

After my time at Sweetwater today, Elise pulled us up to the busy mall on the suburban outskirts of the city. With the endless rows of cars, I could tell it was a busy time at the mall, even though it was a weeknight. This place had everything: urban shoe stores, department clothing stores, and family-owned businesses.

Finally, we reached our intended destination. The only slightly gothic store in the mall. Dark Hearts Boutique. Heavy screamo music blared out of the tunnel-like entrance. A wide array of Tim Burton memorabilia, Halloween costumes, and gothic attire lined the black and red walls. *This* I would say was one of my only favorite stores in the mall. Elise pointed up to a cute strapless dress hanging up on the wall.

"Look at that," she exclaimed, pulling my arm to draw my attention to it. The dress was black with a pewter bat on the neckline.

Immediately, I imagined myself wearing it with Kris. I would waltz inside the clan room wearing it, captivating the attention of every clan member, Valentin included. Vivid would fume. Kris would fall under my spell.

"Now *that* would be perfect for Halloween this year," I replied to Elise with a grin.

Then what I had forgotten about smacked me in the face. I was going to have to tell her I wouldn't be with her on Halloween. In fact, I didn't even know where I would be on Halloween. How was I going to do this to her? I pulled Elise's arm to another corner of the store to admire more things. Distracting her with the cute, captioned t-shirts. I collected some Nightmare Before Christmas memorabilia on sale for Halloween, while Elise continued to admire the vinyl t-shirts displayed across the back wall. I plopped my stuff down at the check-out counter.

"Wait." Elise paused, glancing back to the front of the store. "Would you like to try on that dress?"

My chest tightened. I didn't even think about this either. Elise would see the cut from the night Kris drank from me. I wanted her to believe I was still doing good with my cutting addiction.

"No, I'm okay," I said after hesitating a bit.

"C'mon, Dalia. It's perfect for you. I'll buy it!" she chimed.

I stood there stunned. Where did this come from? Did she feel she needed to do this to keep me as a friend? The lady behind the register pulled a large rod with a hook to get the dress down from the wall.

"Here you go." With that, she led us to a metal dressing room. Elise and I went in, and I immediately turned to pull off my sweater as Elise took the dress off the hanger. Maybe if I stayed over here, she wouldn't notice it. I looked down at the cut on my arm and saw it was still very fresh. I cringed as I pulled my sweater off. It was still sore. But Elise still was distracted by the dress. Okay, good.

"Here, you can just hand it to me," she said, reaching for the sweater.

I didn't dare turn my body around. Elise handed the dress over but then paused. I turned my head around to see her. She was staring directly at my arm.

"Dalia ..." She put the dress down on the bench nearby as she reached for my arm.

She examined the wound intently, then frantically grabbed my other arm; my scars were not as fresh but still visible.

"Are you...?" she trailed off, unable to speak.

"It's not what you think," I interrupted her, biting my lip.

"I thought you were doing better." Her mouth quivered.

"I was! I am." I pointed at my fresh wound. "This isn't from me, it's from Kris."

Her eyes got wider than before, and her jaw dropped. "What? Why? I mean... how?" she stuttered, and her eyes filled with tears.

"It's not what you think, Elise." I pulled my arm away, lowering my gaze in shame. "Kris drank blood from me for the first time last week. It's what the clan does."

She didn't look any less shocked or upset. "Why? What does this clan do anyway?"

That's a question I asked myself quite a lot recently.

"I mean, I understand the whole vampire niche, but isn't that a little abusive? Did you want him to?" Her expression, if anything, only hardened.

"Yes," I responded quickly. "I wanted him to."

Elise just stared at me. It was a lie but my best defense at this point.

162

Taking a breath, I said, "Let me try on the dress." I pointed at it.

We continued in silence as she helped me zip it up. It fit me perfectly.

"I'm buying this for Halloween," I said quietly.

"That's perfect, Dalia. I can't wait to go trick or treating..." I looked down at the ground.

There was still silence, a tension hanging in the air that clawed at both of us. I was going to have to tell her.

"Elise... I think I will be with Kris for Halloween this year," I mumbled.

How could I possibly tell her about the ceremony, the initiation? In between sleeping in a coffin and drinking blood, I wouldn't have time for our usual innocent trick-or-treating. Elise just stared at me and held my arm gently. She placed her shaking hand on the cut.

Finally, she spoke with her eyes dead set on mine, "Kris is killing you." The fitting room door clanged shut as she walked out.

Elise and I were quiet on the ride back to my house. It was like many rides we had recently. How would I fix this mess? I wasn't sure if I could. I loved Kris too much to just let him go. Elise would understand someday, right? If she found a love like this, she would understand.

As we pulled up to my house, I noticed a light blue Mustang in the driveway. My heart ached, and I inhaled sharply. Now this?

"My mom is here." I quickly pulled my seat belt off.

Elise grabbed my hand. "Wait."

I stammered, "Elise... I'm not sure what—"

"Look, it's okay." she interrupted. She looked deep into my eyes with her pale blue ones, innocence, and love in her gaze. "I'm just worried about you. If you want to reconsider and still want to go trick or treating with me this Halloween, I'm still here."

I held her hand until my palm began to sweat. How could I fix this? I wish it were possible to mesh her world with the clan's world. I didn't want to lose Elise, and I didn't want to lose Kris. I wanted to just blurt out everything to her right now. I wanted to cry and have her hold me and tell me she wanted me to marry Kris. I wanted to invite her to the ceremony. But I couldn't.

"I will try." I let her hand go and stepped out of the car, and at the same time, I felt like I was losing her. I was losing my best friend. I walked up the driveway with a bit of hesitation. Knowing that what I was about to face may not be pleasant either. The last time I had talked to my mother, it didn't turn out well. My mom flung the door open as soon as I reached the porch. Her arms encapsulated me before I even took a breath to say hello. Her hair smelled of rosemary and smoke. The grip around me caused the amulet to dig in between my chest.

"Hi! I wasn't expecting you to be here," I muttered as her arms crushed me.

"Awe, come in dear." She held my hand as we walked into the house and shut the door. "You've got a new friend, I hear." Mom winked at me as I let go of her hand. "Oh, and where did you get this?"

She squinted towards me and touched the blood-red amulet around my neck. I tried not to flinch.

"From my friend." I rolled my eyes and turned to walk down the hall to my bedroom, trying to keep my breathing steady and calm.

Why did this have to happen now? Now of all times, she came for a family reunion?

Mom trailed behind me and stood next to my vanity mirror as I plopped down on my bed. Why did she have to intrude so much? That was one thing I enjoyed about living with Dad. He never really got into my business much.

164

"So, how did you meet this friend? Is he a boy?" Mom inquired as she sat down on the bed next to me, grinning wide.

I glanced into my vanity mirror across from me, watching my face to make sure I didn't slip up in my words or my expression. She could always tell when I was lying, so I would keep the conversation short and dry.

"At rehab and no," I said briskly with a shrug. I didn't want to tell her everything. She wouldn't even become aware that soon, I would be a vampire bride.

A small laugh escaped from her. "Okay, dear." She stopped eyeing me for a minute. "Just make sure you are being careful, and you are making the right decisions."

My head snapped towards her. "What 'decisions' do you think I'm making exactly?" I glared at her as blood rushed to my face.

She had only been here a few minutes, and I was already mad. She thought she could just waltz in here and give me all the wisdom of a perfect mom. Maybe she figured she couldn't get any more information from me and tried to upset me instead. I knew that she already had preconceived ideas about love because of what happened between her and dad. She sighed and gently put her hand on my shoulder. It was warm to the touch, but to me, it was a cold reminder of our lack of relationship.

I stared back up into her eyes. They were ragged and drained. Filled with the disappointment of life, of what could happen when love was gone and empty. The divorce, I knew, left her that way.

"You know what I mean." The words fell from her lips with the trailing pain of her split-up, torn-apart life.

"Okay," I replied and attempted to calm myself down.

She tenderly kissed my forehead and walked towards my bedroom door. "I'll see you again soon." With that, she disappeared down the hall.

Minutes later, her light blue Mustang peeled out of the drive-way as she left for who knew how long this time. Tears crossed my cheeks as I pressed my hand against the fogged-up bedroom window. This fear loomed within me, reminding me of the pain I could not forget from the night she first left. This was something I didn't want to face. Could my love with Kris fade away? I knew for a fact that what Kris and I had was real. I was ready to tie my soul to his.

Chapter
Twenty-Eight
Devil's Night

EVERYTHING WAS GOING TO change, and I had to be ready. October 30th. "Devil's Night" is what I called it. Tonight was my initiation, my new birth to a new name, a new world, a new state of being. I sat down on my bed and looked up at the portrait that Kris had given me. An urge to numb the pain with my own swept through me. A swirl of thoughts rushed through my mind, and my body began to shake. These dreams that had been haunting me, plaguing me lately had been enough of a sign. Was this the right decision?

No, I couldn't have a panic attack on the night of my initiation. I had to be strong right now. Tentatively, I picked up the small razor blade next to the candle on my nightstand. My hand trembled as I placed the blade on my wrist. My phone vibrated on my bed, distracting me from what I was about to do.

"Can I pick you up now?" Kris texted.

I glared down at the blade and clenched my teeth. I didn't want to come back to this. My sick habit cut away my pain. Kris would be my cure. I had never felt accepted as much as I did in his arms.

"Yes." I replied to his text.

"Look outside," he typed back.

Bright lights flashed through my dark black curtains. He was here already! I pulled on a pair of jeans, a tank top, and a hoodie to keep me warm from the chilly October air. I just hoped that my dad would think I was going out with Elise. He hadn't made a noise or even acknowledged I was home. Maybe he wouldn't even notice I was gone. The star-filled night sky and cool breeze met me as I stepped out the front door. Even more pleasant than the stars above us was Kris as he opened the car door for me.

"My dad didn't even notice I left," I said as I buckled my seat-belt.

"You're so bad now." Kris smiled as he kissed my hand in his.

His eyes brighter as he looked into mine. Was it the full moon shining on him that made him look sexier?

"Let's go to the cave, and you can get ready for tonight, my love" He gently closed my car door behind me.

I looked down at my arm. It only had the one fresh cut from Kris drinking from my flesh. If Kris wasn't here at this moment, I would have given in to my urge to cut. A warm sensation filled my heart. This was right for me. He was my cure.

"Your scars can have purpose now." His smooth voice replayed in my head. The night he drank from me cured me.

My shoulders peeked out from the long, pressed dress and fit perfectly around my waist and flowed as I walked. Rubies around my neckline matched the hue of my deep red lips. Zayn braided my hair so half of it flowed down my shoulders, leaving a couple of wisps out to frame my face. She also placed black diamond earrings on my ears. My hands shook as I looked into the mirror.

Biting my lip, I observed my last couple moments before I joined the clan. Zayn gently touched my hand.

"Are you ready for tonight?" Zayn asked quietly.

There was no going back now. The commotion of the Garden District slowed as midnight approached. Dressed in my wedding gown, I uncomfortably sat in the leather seat of Alex's Mercedes as we drove along. The growing silence between Alex and I remained, only serving to trigger my anxiety even more. If only I could have something to distract myself?

My eyes glanced up out of the window. I noticed the full moon as I looked out at the empty streets. It was a clear night. The moonlight shone much like it did the night Kris took me to the fire baptism. That night was one I would always remember. It's like my eyes were opened to a whole new world. An elusive vampire world filled with Kris and the clan. It was a world full of beauty and mystery. My heart pounded as Alex pulled into the old cemetery gate and through the graves.

Anticipation rose with each gravestone we passed as the metal wiring of my corset kept me from taking in a deeper breath. Only the sound of gravel crushing under the car's tires remained between Alex and me. He stopped the car close to the old, stone gazebo and turned his lights off. The moment when I placed a bouquet on Lestat's memorial flashed through my memory as I clenched the red roses in my hands now. I paused for a moment before placing my hand on the car's door handle. What if the love between Kris and I did not last? Would it end in death just as the flowers?

I turned to look out the window as we got closer to our destination. Tall candelabras lined the narrow path leading up to the graveyard gazebo. The very place Kris had proposed to me. This was my place of solitude and many nights, it was also my place of salvation. I would lay my life into his and his into mine. We would be united for eternity. The very thought settled every negative emotion within me.

Slowly, I stepped out of the car, and Kris gleamed when he saw me. The smell of earth and water filled the air, signaling the coming rain. The graveyard's shifted dirt held no mercy as the tattered train from my dress dragged along, covering the ground with every step I took toward Kris.

Silence filled the air again, but this time it gave me peace. I walked down the pathway lined with candles. Heat rushed to my face as I looked up to see Kris dressed in an all-black suit. His face shone in the moonlight as he beamed down at me. *I'm doing this. I'm really doing this.* Kris's fangs revealed within his bright smile as he extended his hand to me. His eyes expressed nothing but pleasure.

Nothing but the moonlight and candles that encircled us provided us light, offering a shadowy and harrowing ambiance for the wedding. Kris placed my hand in his and gazed longingly into my eyes.

"I love you, my bride," the words flowed smoothly from his lips. He motioned to Alex standing a few feet away.

"Let's begin the initiation," Alex proclaimed.

I could feel my heart pounding in my chest. Kris looked magnificent tonight. His hair was slicked over and edged neatly down by his shoulders; his pale skin illuminated by the candle's flickering flames surrounding us. His cheekbones well defined by the dimmed light. The atmosphere gave a perfect mix of darkness.

His fangs peeked out through his timid smile. My own lips tingled with the sensation of my imagination. Much like before, I wanted him to hold me in his arms and never let go.

"Dalia, my family is here only to witness the beauty we will bestow upon them tonight. We stand before them and the Devil himself as we become one being," Kris said to me.

I breathed in deeply. The musky cemetery air filled my lungs, reminding me of the sweet taste of immortality before me. Being here alone for many years, longing for death, envying every corpse in their grave had prepared me for this. I looked solely into his deep eyes. I could find what I wanted in him.

"I'm ready," I replied, raising my chin.

Kris looked deeper into my eyes. Deeper than ever before. They pulled me into a trance.

"Dalia, we will be joined in death, so we can be joined in life. This can only be done by blood. The very life within our veins."

He held up a small blade in his hand.

"Will you take my life?" he said reverently.

"I will." Every second felt as if eternity had passed as soon as the words left my lips.

Kris etched the blade across his wrist. Blood leaked from the wound and onto his hand, and he cupped his bloodied hand onto my chest. Covering the amulet adorning my neck with his blood.

"Then my blood will cover you, and you will be mine," he stated. My eyes could not stray from Kris as he spoke, and my breath became heavy.

The sacredness of the moment left me speechless. Kris continued his vows as he lifted the silver goblet, plunging the blade deeper into his arm. His face twisted in pain as he used his strength to go deep enough to hit the vein beneath. The blood from him flowed out and into the chalice. My eyes began to tear up, seeing him violently extract his own blood for me.

Kris, using his other hand to grab mine, peered into my eyes and asked, "Dalia, will you drink and be filled with my love... for an eternity?"

"I will," I swore, and he raised the chalice mixed with his blood.

"As my bride, will you give me your life, your blood?" He squeezed my hand. "Will you join me in death so we will become one for eternity?"

I kept my gaze on his eyes, waiting for my thoughts to form into words. I knew he was waiting for my reply, but this had been a lifelong dream of mine coming true. I opened my mouth to give him my response as the final nail in the coffin.

"You can have my life, my blood. It's yours." I leaned back my head to reveal my neck, unshielded and given to him completely. "I am your bride," I said confidently.

Kris placed the blade against my neck as I turned my head away from him and toward the red rose terrace. The blade sunk deep into my skin and withdrew blood. I winced as I endured the sharp pain of the knife cutting my flesh and dragging through the tissues. He pressed the blade deeper until a small stream flowed down to my chest. Then Kris leaned into me, his breath hovering above my gaping neck. Licking his lips, he plunged in. His fangs pulled as his mouth met my skin. The smell of blood and his cologne mixed as he wrapped his arms around me.

He was drawing life from my veins and vehemently continued to suck from my wound. No matter how beautiful this looked in Hollywood films, it was nothing like real life. This was ethereal. Kris came up for a breath of air. His lips dripped with my blood as he looked down at me. I could no longer contain myself. I grasped his face in my hands and pulled my forehead onto his. Our eyes only met for a second before I went in and kissed him, my lips trembling as they caressed the blood.

His arms wrapped around me, and his body enveloped mine. Our breath intertwined with every second our lips touched. I had laid my soul before Kris. I am united with the clan.

Chapter
Twenty-Nine

Twilight
Garden

WE WERE NO LONGER alone. Cloaked figures walked in a circular form, transcending out from the shadows of the tombstones. They were walking towards the gazebo, each one holding long flickering torches. I turned to see them from every side of the gazebo. Did the clan come to witness the wedding? Or was this something Valentin planned? Fear began to rise within me. Had I been tricked? The threat rose within me before I could speak. What if Valentin was here?

Kris saw the panic in my eyes. He hurried to reassure me, "No worries, my dear, they are just here to witness the final act."

"What are they doing?' I looked back up into his trusting eyes.

But Kris was silent as he led me out of the gazebo. Alex pulled a black hooded cloak over himself.

"Wait." I pulled my arm from his. He calmed my nerves as he put my hand back into his and whispered into my ear. "Drink and be filled." He stood there with the silver chalice in his hand.

He raised the chalice to my lips. It happened as it did before when I drank blood. The intoxicating power of the blood filled my being. My spirit lifted, and my body felt empowered. Now when I drank of the blood, this... *life* surged within me. I stared back into Kris's eyes as he took the chalice away. He, too, could tell the difference within me. His thumb caressed my chin below my bloodied lips as he kissed me.

The clan drew closer to us, surrounding us from each side. Alex, standing next to Kris, held a satisfied grin on his face. The cloaked clan members came out from the shadows and began to congratulate us one by one. Many of them hugged me. This was my family now. Kris embraced me tenderly from behind. His chest against my back made me feel safe. Even with a vampire clan in the graveyard at midnight.

"You are a part of us, a part of me," Kris whispered into my ear as my heart leapt with joy.

I belonged. Zayn was the last one to hug me. Her embrace was full of warmth and love. She was like my mother to me now. I didn't feel the hollow emptiness or bitter upset as I did with my biological mom.

"You did so great, my dear." She pushed a strand of my hair back behind my ear. "And you looked so beautiful."

I beamed back at her as Kris grabbed my hand. The cloaked clan members walked back into the shadows of the graveyard as he and I stepped into the black Mercedes to return to the Batcave.

"We will finish the night here." Kris led me through the darkness that seemed to arise from the dance floor at the Batcave.

The DJ's haunting voice bellowed from the speakers as each body swayed with an enchanting form. The scent of incense, alcohol, and cigarettes filled the foggy air. The industrial beats pounding through the club room sang to my very being. The music reverberating united and moved my body along with Kris.

"Eternity.Eternity." The song chanted.

My body frail as bumps formed on the back of my arms. I knew the answer to the question. I had found Kris; this *was* my eternity. Kris and I thrashed our bodies along with the clan.

At one point, I pinched my arm to make sure I wasn't just dreaming. For years, I had dreamed of falling in love. I would find a vampire knight to love me and be immortal with. Kris looked deep into my eyes as he gently pulled me around him. As the music came to an end, Kris grabbed my hand.

"My vampire bride." He kissed me proudly.

We maneuvered through the crowd of clubgoers, making our way to the red booths next to the bar. I had just experienced the greatest high of my life. The red lights from the bar shone onto his pale skin. They reflected mystery into his eyes that I loved. Kris led me to the booth that I almost sat in the first night I came to the Batcave. With everything that had transpired since then, it felt nostalgic to sit here. I felt my heart flutter with joy and an unspeakable feeling of love.

"Two drinks." Kris waved at the bartender. She nodded at him and began creating the concoctions behind the counter. He turned to me. "What would you like to do now that you're my vampire bride?"

"I just want to be with you," I said simply, sighing with content.

He grinned. "Definitely."

The bartender came and placed our drinks on our table before disappearing back behind the bar to grab her half-smoked cigarette from a waiting ashtray. I reached over the table to hold Kris's hand. We were perfect. Two young gothic bats in love as we sipped on our straws and stared at each other with the same glazed-over, dreamy look. My Bloody Mary was nothing like the bloody drinks we had in the clan room. A pungent tomato taste with a sting of liquor coated my mouth as I sipped it down.

"This is all ours now. When Zayn and Alex retire, this is ours," Kris said as I scanned around the clubroom.

I indeed felt powerful, but not because of my drink. Because I was the queen over this. I turned toward Kris, who was still staring at me. Heat rushed to my face as I smiled at him. I tried to just keep my cool amidst this world so unfamiliar to me. But then an unpleasant face appeared in the corner of my eye. Valentin and Vivid were standing across the dance floor. His face looked like someone he loved had just died.

"Look over there." I pointed discreetly over to them.

"I've never seen Valentin look so... defeated," Kris sipped the last of his drink. Then he stood, offering his hand to me. "Let's go to my coffin now before Valentin gets some crazy idea. Leave the rest of the celebrating to these ghouls."

I flinched. His coffin; I had forgotten about that part. I was to sleep in it tonight.

"Are you okay?" he asked, noticing my troubled expression.

"Yes." I pulled myself out of the booth and plastered on a smile. The alcohol from the drink made my stomach turn a bit more than usual, but fake it till you make it, right?

"Are you ready?" Kris replied.

"Yes, I am." I put my hand in his, and he whisked me away. Just like Alex did the first time I stood by this club booth.

Chapter Thirty
Eternal
Flames

DEEP RED ROSES SURROUNDED the coffin. My black lace gloves trailed along the wood as I bit my lip. This was my fate. Why would I be afraid to face it? Lying to rot in a coffin was everyone's fate, after all. Why would it scare us? Why would it cause any hesitation? If anything, this should be the most relieving moment. A moment when time stopped. Work would end, and turmoil finally came to a halt. The last breath has been given, and your soul can finally rest. *This was what I wanted.*

But why was it that when I met fate, my heart pounded even more? Kris slowly creaked open the wooden coffin in the corner of his room.

"I slept in here the first night of my initiation. It's for you now, Dalia. Your first night in the coffin." Kris smiled at me.

I traced the deep red velvet lining with my gloved fingertips. I was happy that I had become an immortal, a night creature along with Kris. Yet I was hesitant about this. Perhaps because this coffin resembled the one in my dream with the knight?

"Don't worry, Dalia. I'll be sleeping in here with you. If anything happens, I'll be right here." Kris's hand pressed against my shoulder reassured me.

Moonbeams that streamed in from the window crossed my face as I stepped into the coffin and gently laid down. My entire body had a sense of urgency to get out, yet my mind pressed me to go in. I kept my lips tightly shut. I must not ruin this now. Kris lit white votives around the coffin. Anxiety panged through my chest each time he lit a new candle. I closed my eyes and tried to calm my nerves. Finally, he slid his soft hand across my temple and down across my cheek. His touch put me at ease, and I took a deep breath.

"Dalia," he said. I opened my eyes. "This is hard on the first night. It's a bit different, but you will get comfortable. That's why I gave you that Bloody Mary." He smirked.

This coffin lid creaked as it enclosed on me. This was it.

I was met with this finally. Darkness surrounded me. The only sensation left was the beating of the dark wave music still pulsing in the background. The heat of my own body was trapped inside as well. My heart beat faster as I clenched my fists and closed my eyes. I could do this. Sweat formed within my hands and along my neck.

I breathed in, as this was the only thing that could calm me along with listening to the music reverberating outside of my confinement. This made me a vampire badass bride, right? I shut my eyes tight. Sleeping in here was the last nail in the coffin.

179

The sensation of death filled my veins. Blood pooling down in my body as my heart stopped. The warmth from my hands escaped me. Cold, lifeless, and rotting. My cheeks sunk in, and my skin shriveled. Who did this to me? I looked at myself as if I was outside of myself. Was I truly dead? What happened? My heart had stopped. I was here, in my death. The coffin surrounded me and only confirmed that I was indeed deceased.

Then, in the darkness, something clicked. The wooden coffin jolted. The humid air inside the confined space, the one that had helped me rot, was met with a stark cold breeze. How did I feel about this? Beams of light revealed a rotted, disgusting body. *My* body. Why could I see myself outside of myself?

Blood rushed within my veins. Sinew tied together, now restored. My skin became baby-soft again. The sound of bones cracking back into place made me gasp. I opened my eyes to see *him*. Fire in his eyes.

Still, I was in a frozen state of shock. I looked down at the opened coffin, seeing not a corpse but the figure of a beaming bride. I was in the same wedding hall as before. The figure I had encountered then inched closer from the darkness surrounding me. The knight. I was here again. I could not breathe, and my hand clung to the side of the coffin. A warmth that contrasted the cold I felt, the only thing I felt, met my lips. Fear filled my heart until a sudden peace rushed over me. A jolting power rushed through me. A beating like a drum filled my ears. Air rushed into my lungs, and I gasped.

"I love you, Dalia. You can live, because I live," the knight whispered.

I turned towards the knight to reply, but his eyes still were nothing but flames.

"Dalia. What will you choose?" His voice echoed.

The coffin burst into flames. I jumped away as a high-pitched tone pierced through my ears. My head pounded, and darkness surrounded me. I gasped, breathing in with everything I had. Sweat and tears began to stream my face as I pushed at the barrier surrounding me. *I'm here. I'm in the darkness again.* Music pounded on the outside this darkness. I was in the coffin once more. I pounded harder, kicking the wood only inches from my face. I *must* get out. I thrashed my body. *I can't be here.*

I breathed in heavily and used all my strength to push on the heavy wooden door. This time, when the door flung open, Kris was above me with concern in his eyes. Tears continued to stream down my cheeks as I sat up and covered my face. My body moved up with my knees to my chest. My nails dug deep into my thighs as Kris tenderly wrapped his arms around me, covering my shoulder and placing my head into his chest.

"Dalia, it's okay. Are you alright?" He pulled my hands from my face.

I was too ashamed of what had happened. The flames of the white candles that he lit surrounding the coffin had died off. The coffin wasn't on fire. The knight wasn't here, only Kris.

"I'm fine." I wiped the tears from my face.

He strung his arm under my knees and back and scooped me out from the silky red coffin. My body shifted into his as he picked me up. Relief filled me as I rested against his chest. I set my eyes over his broad shoulder and stared at one small candle still lit beside the coffin. It danced, casting shadows on the wood.

Kris pulled me away from him. "What's wrong?" he asked.

I hid my face from him. I couldn't show him my fear. "I just had a bad dream, and the coffin made me claustrophobic."

"You can sleep in my bed." He placed me like a ragdoll onto the back corner of his bed. Then he wrapped his body around mine and wiped the sweat that glistened across my forehead.

My tensed muscles relaxed, my jaw unclenched, and my heartbeat slowed as I calmed myself. Cocooned between a black comforter and his strong arms, I felt safe. Warmth filled my body and my soul. I felt his love surrounding me. But who was this knight? He seemed to have the same passionate pursuit for me as Kris. His fire seemed untamable. The dancing flames on the last candle taunted me as I fell asleep. Reminding me, the knight had eyes of fire.

Chapter
Thirty-One
The Prey

THE RAIN BEATING ON the small window outside matched my soul. Heavy. I wiggled around in the soft blankets surrounding me with Kris's warm body lying next to mine. His smooth, rhythmic breathing caused his chest to rise and lower against my back. I turned in the covers to look at his face directly. Even as he slept, he looked so perfect. How did I deserve someone like him?

My body pressed against his chest as I set my lips on his and kissed him. He barely flinched. A heavy sleeper, I guess. My head tingled as I slowly stood up. Throbbing pain from last night rushed through my head, and I was slightly dizzy as my vision faded in and out. My knees slightly buckled as my feet met the cold cement floor. The chair next to the mattress steadied me as I grabbed it.

I cradled my hand against my forehead and waited for my body to catch its balance. Was I still faint from the blood loss? I ran my hand through my hair. Turning around, I faced the thing that haunted my dreams last night. Before my eyes was the chilling figure of the coffin in the corner.

I distracted myself from it by walking towards a full-body mirror in the opposite corner. The small cut on my neck from the vow I made last night was still fresh as I placed my hand on it. My finger traced the wound. I gave myself one last glance in my black gown that I somehow managed to sleep in. My makeup was smeared across my face.

I didn't want Kris to see me like this. I needed to go home and at least shower. I tugged my wedding dress off and onto the floor. Striped to my underwear, I ran over to a pile of Kris's clothes on the floor.

A black cotton t-shirt caught my eye. I grabbed it and pulled it over my head. It fit me loosely, just covering my bottom. I tugged the shirt down, and the fibers hugged my body, but then I pulled the neck up to my nose. I inhaled his heavenly smell, which intoxicated me as I breathed in deep. A deep aroma mixed with sage incense and the scent of his soft skin.

I jumped as a chill went up my bare feet and to my core. I needed something else besides his t-shirt to wear, and I was smelling his clothes. Imagine if he woke up to me doing that. I searched around the room until I noticed a pile of clothes by the door. The jeans I came to the Batcave in were there. How did they get there? I scurried across the room to pick them up.

Zayn must have brought them in here for me. She was kind enough to do something like that. I pulled myself into them quickly as Kris still slept. He looked sexy as he laid across the mattress halfway covered by the comforter. I pulled myself from staring too long. *Focus, Dalia.*

Opening the bedroom door, I began to walk down the quiet red hallway. The silence was a drastic change compared to the normal club beats that filled the space. I hoped none of the members would see me leaving. Especially Valentin. But a distant voice in the club room intrigued me. I opened the black door to enter the Batcave's dance floor. Alex was standing there next to Elvira 2.0 as I opened the door. He looked surprised to see me, like the other times I showed up at the club unannounced.

"Dalia?"

"Want a smoke?" He offered me a pack of Marlboro Reds.

I pulled a cigarette out of the pack, glancing down at it and biting my lip. I'd never smoked before.

"Oh, you don't want to get her started on those!" Elvira 2.0 batted her long fake lashes and snatched the cigarette box from him. She pulled out one for herself and lit it.

He chuckled. "She isn't as young as you think, dear."

Elvira handed me the zippo lighter she had just used with a shrug.

"What do you need, darling?" She dragged on her cigarette after speaking.

Here goes nothing. I took my first hit. Choking a bit yet trying to pretend that the toxic fumes didn't bother me, I went ahead and asked Alex, "Can I have a ride home?"

He raised a brow at me. "It's raining pretty hard out there. Are you sure you don't want to wait for Kris?"

"Yes, I'm sure." I nodded. "My dad is probably wondering where I'm at."

He motioned Elvira towards the back hidden door. "Alright, anything for you, dear. I'll let Kris know when he wakes up. Whenever that will be," he stated matter-of-factly as we both walked towards his car waiting outside the club. The rain outside seemed to drown out any conversation Alex and I could have had. The drops against the car window pounded like my heart did last night. *Thump-thump-thump.* It was deafening.

Once we reached my house, Alex firmly grasped my hand. "Dalia, remember what we talked about? This cannot be removed or revoked. You're one of us now."

I nodded, the weight of his words on me. "I'll be back at the club later tonight." *Thump-thump*.

Alex nodded in return, waiting for me to exit the car through the thunderstorm. The walk up to my home felt unnatural after last night. I wondered when I would be able to stay at the Batcave with Kris permanently. I could run away, maybe conveniently disappear? I cringed as soon as I touched the doorknob to the front door, my hands slippery from the rain. I forgot I needed to hide the cut on my neck from last night. I hurriedly searched my bag to find my choker necklace and wrapped it around the cut from last night's ceremony. My skin burned as the cloth rubbed against the open wound.

The doorknob jangled. Oh crap! I jumped back. Was that...? It proved scarier than what I thought was standing above me. Not Valentin, seeking revenge for last night's escapade. Instead, my dad loomed over me this time when the door opened. A worried expression covered his face. One I had become familiar with by now.

"What are you doing, Dalia? I didn't see you come home last night." He grabbed my arm and tugged me inside.

I glanced back through the downpour. Alex had already driven away. *That's a good thing*.

Dad leaned his nose to my shoulder after shutting the door and patting my shoulders dry. "You smell like... dirt?" His expression turned perplexed.

"Elise and I went to the graveyard last night to read poetry for Halloween!" I blurted out the first thing I could make up. I hated lying to him, and it didn't seem to really convince him.

But he only shrugged and turned away. "I guess I can't say I never had my fair share of weird Halloween celebrations as a teen."

He began to walk down the hallway towards his room. *That's it?* It was that easy? He didn't even ask another question. This time, though, I was intrigued.

I chased him down the hall. "What do you mean, Dad?"

He stopped in front of his bedroom door and turned. The game in the background on the TV called to him, beckoning him back to his recliner. I knew it. His eyes seemed distracted even as he looked at me.

"What do you mean by... *you did weird things for Halloween*?" I prodded him.

I was curious about his teen years. Did he have the same fascination with the dark side as I did, but it was hidden beneath years of adult responsibility? As far as I knew, him and Mom were the classic football player and cheerleader couple. They were top of their class, homecoming king and queen normies. I was the only odd one in this family.

He snorted. "Oh, I used to do much worse than reading poetry in the graveyard. Stuff you should never know about."

My mind raced with questions, and my mouth turned to the side.

"Really?" I touched my chin.

"I've got to catch the game, kid." He quickly turned and vanished into his room, shutting the door in my face.

My body trembled at the thought about my dad, and if he would ever know what happened with Kris and I last night. He didn't though. A numbing pain on my neck from the choker rubbing against the wound ended my bout of reflection. I went into the bathroom and locked the door behind me. Yanking off the choker, I splashed the wound with cold water. This was worse than when I inflicted pain on myself.

I stared deep into the same mirror I looked in right before leaving last night. But now, I was different. My eyes looked darker. Maybe there was some significance in what Kris believed in. I was an immortal being now. I felt different, too. I took a cool shower that swept away any residue from the ceremony and locked myself back into my own little cave to rest. How did the past few weeks lead up to this? An eternal vow to Kris.

I pulled the sheet on my bed over my body and sighed. The flurry of events made me dizzy like the lack of blood after last night's ceremony. Did Kris wake up yet? My phone had a blank screen. No notifications. Elise had not texted me either. My headache only got worse as I thought about it. How could I bring our friendship back together?

I stretched my body across my mattress and stared up at the painting hanging above my bed. The painting with the man holding the woman below him. His fangs ready and mouth open, about to consume her. To kill her. The phrase from the mall that Elise said plunged into my chest.

"Kris is killing you."

I had always seen the beauty in vampire romance. Now I suddenly realized the twinge of sadistic perversity. The man hung over the woman in a domineering way, his fangs ready to sink deep into the girl's neck, just like Kris did with me. Was I the victim of a sick game called love? Was this what Kris and I had? I pressed on the wound on my neck Kris sucked my blood from. Was I in the same kind of love with Kris?

The thing that had kept me alive in the midst of pain was the idea of true love. I had always wanted a vampire lover to come and take me from my grave of despair. Kris had done that. He awoke me out of the monotony of the real world and into a dark world of beauty. Something eternal and real. But was that something even true or possible? If I were to die, would I wake up as an immortal being? The belief Kris had wasn't fully convincing to me yet.

I looked up to my painting of the romantic vampire holding his prey. The young girl that had fallen into his arms. She was the one he could suck the life out of. There was no beauty in that. The only real thing I could find was in the blade with myself. The girl in the painting hadn't found true love. She had become the victim to an evil man's deception. Was it possible that the love I found with Kris was a deception as well?

I turned towards my mirror and began to wipe away my make-up from last night off. I couldn't help but look at the bright red cuts all over me. My stomach began to turn at the sight of them. Elise was right. How did I get to this point? I searched for my phone. I had to call her now. But then I paused. I couldn't. This was too hard.

What would I tell her? I still had to be with Kris tonight. Being with him and the clan wasn't exactly something I could just back out of. Emotions flooded my body, and I turned towards my vanity. Where was my blade? I scraped around looking under things for it. I didn't want to come back to this, but I found the small blade under my makeup compact. I switched on a light and some rock music for the background so my dad wouldn't suspect anything.

Lighting the candle to burn the blade flooded me with mem-ories from last night. The candles surrounding the coffin and the dream with the knight. These dreams that had been haunting me the past few weeks should have been enough of a sign to me. I should have known they meant something. Joining the clan was a mistake. The fear that I felt as I laid within that coffin last night entered me again. It paralyzed my soul.

I broke my remorse as the blade traced my arm and blood leaked free. Kris said that my blood was worth something. It was valuable to him, at least. Not to me. I dragged the blade across my arm one more time and felt the rush. The exhilaration of inflicting pain on myself flowed through my body. I shut my eyes to match the oblivion my body delved into. An image entered the darkness as I closed them. The knight's fiery eyes met mine. A cup in his hand, with blood, offered to me. I jumped and caught myself, realizing I was still here and not in a dream. Who was this knight that had plagued my dreams?

There had to be a real reason behind it. I knew people could send a spell to give a person nightmares. I was superstitious enough to believe that Valentin could be sending these dreams. I placed a small washcloth on my cut-up arm and laid down on my bed to let the blood continue to flow from my veins. The music in the background continued to play, echoing the same song of deep pain that dwelled within my heart.

There had to be something that was true. Something real about my love with Kris. I pushed myself up from my bed, and a light stream of blood drifted down my arm. It glided across the cut Kris had made on my arm. The stream of blood crossed the wound, making the figure of a cross on my forearm. The cross?

I rushed over to my bookshelf and snatched a small leather-bound family bible from the top shelf. I kept this bible simply for the beautiful gold marks that etched across the black leather case. Blowing the dust off the cover, I flipped through the pages. The living sacrifice? The crucifix that hung from Valentin's neck rolled through my mind. I chunked the large gold foil-lined pages until I reached the concordance in the back of the book. There had to be some connection with all of this, right?

Blood. My fingers traced the micro-sized text at the bottom of the page. I flipped to Leviticus. Yet again the phrase I found before about blood.

"Leviticus 17:11, For the life of a creature is in the blood."

Anything more? I turned to a place that referenced blood as well. The book of Matthew. The red letters stood out to me.

"Whoever eats my flesh and drinks my blood, has eternal life, and I will raise him up on the last day. John 6:54"

I glanced back at the painting above me. Was Jesus talking about vampires? This was so different from what I thought Jesus was about. I eagerly turned to yet another passage in reference to blood. Stuck in one place with just my lungs and my heart still moving, I froze as I read the words.

"This is my blood of the covenant, which is poured out for many, for the forgiveness of sins." Matthew 26:26"

Tears began to fill my eyes. I looked down to my arm, where I had cut. Blood was worth something. More than just my life. A covenant could be made with blood. Just as I had made a covenant with Kris last night. My phone buzzed, pulling me from the hypnotizing state this book put me in.

"Ready for tonight?" Kris texted.

Thoughts about the knight, my dreams, and the words I had just read ran through my mind. My arm still pulsed from the wounds I had inflicted on myself. It was the only thing that made me feel alive. I didn't want to answer his text yet.

Was that what it meant? Life is in the blood, as it said in the bible. With all the bloodletting I did on myself and every time it had an intoxicating effect on me. The moments I drank blood gave me the same rush of empowerment. I wrapped up my bleeding arm with a long-sleeve shirt. I needed to get ready again for the Halloween party tonight. I could talk to Kris and tell him what I found in the bible. Maybe the clan knew the secrets to eternal life like Jesus did. It seemed like Kris knew what to believe. Apparently, Jesus knew as well that only through the spilling of blood could life come.

Chapter Thirty-Two

Blood Flowers

THE BATCAVE PULSED AS I stepped into it, not as a shy goth girl but as the Queen of the clan. Halloween night had every imaginable thing going on. Even more so at the Batcave. Every gory, horrific costume paraded the dance floor. Lights strobed throughout the warehouse style building. This was my heaven now. I turned to Kris as he danced with me.

"Come with me?" he pulled my arm. He leaned in to kiss me, his lips just as intoxicating as the night he married me into the clan. Could his love be that of a god? The sacrificial kind?

"But... what about the party?" I questioned him, doubting his motives. Just like the first night here, as he led me down the darkened hallway and to the black door of the clan room.

"Trust me. It's okay if we step away for a minute." His charming smile reflected at me. Whatever it is, it worked. First, I saw a candlelight flickering as Kris opened the door wider. There was a table covered in black lace with two candelabras decadently placed on it.

"For you." Kris's voice whispered into my ear.

Chocolate-covered strawberries sat neatly next to a bottle of wine with two small crystal glasses. He pulled a black wooden chair from the table.

"This is so sweet of you." I sat down in the chair he offered, grinning up at him.

"You're welcome, my love." Picking up a chocolate strawberry, he placed it on my lips.

"Careful there! You don't want to mess up my lipstick."

"I don't care if I do. I might mess it up later anyway." He gave me another kiss. Then he leaned over and picked up the large glass bottle. He tugged off the corkscrew still attached to the top with ease and poured deep red into my glass.

"Our first Halloween night as bride and groom," Kris said softly as he stared into the deep red liquid and then back at me.

I clanged the glass against his in recognition of this sacred first night. The thick red liquid swirled in the glass before I put it to my lips. Drinking in, I tasted the empowering rush of blood. Flowing down my neck, through my soul, and into my very own veins. How did this give me such pleasure? It felt just as it did when I cut myself.

I nestled my head onto Kris's back against his chest. So much has changed since the first night I came here with him. My whole world has changed. My hand glided down his arm to rest in his hand. A rough area on his arm caught my attention. The abrasion felt familiar. I looked down to see the scab from a cut on his arm. The place where he gave blood to me last night.

Memories from my initiation flooded my mind. The chalice with blood held to my lips. Giving me the rush of eternal power I craved. The kiss that sealed my fate with Kris. Even the warmth from each clan member hugging me and congratulating me on my initiation. My heart pounded harder at the thought of this. I still felt an aching emptiness inside me.

There had to be something more. I must be the hardest person in the world to please because discontent still filled my soul. Most years I would be trick or treating with Elise. She normally would dress up as a hippie, a fairy, elf, or even a unicorn. I usually went for a darker costume. A vampire or witch. This Halloween, I wasn't just dressed up as a vampire bride, I *was* one.

In Kris's arms was the best place I could ever be. The faint beating of his heart rang through my ear as I pressed my head against his firm chest. I began to trace Kris's palm with my thumb lightly, and he looked down at me.

"I have something special for you." He took out a single white rose with the top of the petals darkened. I softly traced the petals, and my fingertips became wet. A deep red substance covered my finger. I squinted to look closer. He brushed away the hair from my face and lightly kissed my cheek. I looked at my finger... wait. I peered up at Kris for an explanation. The rose hadn't been stained but rather dipped in blood.

"Is this... blood?" I questioned him.

"Blood flowers. They will never die." He smiled at me. "Life is in the blood."

I suddenly remembered what I thought about earlier, and an empty feeling permeated my soul. It pulled me from the ethereal high of being with Kris and back to the questions that haunted me. Kris put his hand lightly beneath my chin to pull my gaze from the rose to look back into his deep eyes.

"What are you thinking about? You look so intense." He placed his hand on my shoulder. The warmth of it left a sense of ease to run through my body.

"I'm thinking about a bible verse I read earlier," I said with a shrug. "What is the significance of the cross?" My eyes traveled to the upside-down cross seared onto his neck.

Kris weaved his fingers, both of his hands, into a solid fist. His eyes drew back down to the glass filled with blood. He was holding something back. "It's about being a living sacrifice. You only get the cross seared onto your neck when you have fully given your blood to the clan. I did, so I got this." He pointed to the scarred tissue on his neck.

"Living sacrifice?" My tone carried curiosity as my mind rushed to the night that Valentin confronted me in front of the Batcave.

"Why do you ask?" Kris raised the glass to his lips to take another sip, his eyes peering over the rim.

"I want to know the real significance of the cross and blood as it relates to the clan." My eyes set on him.

He stared at me for a long moment. I felt more vulnerable each second longer his eyes pierced into mine. Like with Valentin, I sensed he was breathing me in.

"I want to take you somewhere, Dalia," he finally broke the silence.

He pulled me up from the chair, my body catching up with the movement.

"What about the party? And Alex?"

He smirked with no reply and pulled me outside to a back door of the Batcave I had never seen before. Darkness filled the streets. He led me around the corner with his firm grasp as I stumbled behind him. We trekked through piles of garbage from the bars and clubs surrounding us. Shards of glass from broken bottles cracked beneath my boots as I tried to avoid all the obstacles around us.

My eyes scanned the dark alley that we walked down. Where was he taking me? My breath became heavy just trying to keep up. I almost asked Kris where we were going until I saw his car around the corner.

My brows creased. "Where are we going?" Peering down at my hands as I sat down in the car, I noticed the flower he gave me was still in my hand. The blood on it dripped down to my wrist as I held onto the thorny stalk. Kris sat down in the seat next to me.

"The bloodflowers are a symbol for where we are going tonight. Do you want to know what it means to be immortal? To never die?" he pressed.

"What do you mean?"

"It's Halloween. It's the perfect night for it." He began to drive.

I gripped the rose in my hand tighter. It seemed that Kris had to be driving me a million miles away, but I recognized this area. The Garden District with the quaint coffee shops lined along the busy streets. There was a small clearing of large ancient trees nearby. The oak trees were like a web with their branches, making the forest that much harder to see through. He took my hand with a gentleness in his gaze.

"Dalia..." he paused. "I promise you won't regret it."

"Won't regret what?" I stammered.

Kris opened the car door and I stepped out onto the street. I spotted the cathedral with the crucifix nearby, the one I saw with Elise. A small light shone from the bottom of the cross. Kris stopped under a tall tree near the clearing of trees and looked deeply into my eyes.

He explained, "The cross is a symbol of surrender. Of giving oneself for another."

My voice cracked. "And this means?" The cross I had just looked at by the cathedral made me think harder about it. My heart yearned today to gaze at the cross again and to figure out what the connection to the clan would be.

Kris went on, "It means, the significance of giving blood is the same as giving your life. It's becoming a living sacrifice."

Now, I only wanted to look at Kris. His eyes pulled me into him. He held my hand and lightly placed it on his chest. Feeling the warmth of his heartbeat, I turned myself into his intoxicating being. He walked back towards the trees. The darkness covered us as we walked further into the brush.

"Dalia." His deep voice pulled me closer.

I leaned into him, reaching up to his large frame tower over mine. Two gem-like eyes brought me into a trance as we stood in silence before the words he spoke into my ears.

"Would you be a living sacrifice?"

Chapter Thirty-Three
Living Sacrifice

MOONBEAMS FADED BEHIND THE cloud-filled sky. The air itself was suffocating. I clenched my teeth. The thought of what I was about to do made me anxious, besides the fact that I was being watched. I leaned against the tree nearby and then knelt in the grass. Deep down, I knew there wasn't much worth to my life. I was so used to bloodletting for my own pleasure. If I could give my life for something valuable, I would.

So here I was. I stretched my arm out towards Kris. Still, I never thought this would be the way I'd give my life. He smiled, comforting me with the firmness of his hand holding mine as he grasped a large silver needle in his other hand. I grinned back up at him. The needle didn't bother me. The solemness of what I was about to do did. Kris's expression caused a calmness to come over me. I wanted him more than anything. So this was what I had to do.

I flinched as Kris plunged the needle into my arm. "It's going to be okay. I'm draining the blood now."

The rough bark of the tree grated against my side as I slanted onto the tree harder. Trembling as the blood poured into the chalice, my head spun, and I felt faint. How long would this take? I bowed my head to the ground, and sweat trickled down my temples. The fall air offered little relief to me as it brushed over my body. If this was my sacrifice, I would do it. I was determined to focus on what this meant and why I wanted to do this. This must be what it meant in the bible verse. To become the living sacrifice. I closed my eyes, envisioning the cross in front of the cathedral.

"Are you okay?" Kris asked softly. I opened my eyes to his piercing eyes in front of me and nodded weakly.

Kris seamlessly pulled the needle from my arm. "And done."

Something dropped from his hand and onto the ground as he walked away. The needle that he used to extract my blood fell next to me on the leaves. A large needle with medical tubing attached to it. I winced. Did I see this at a doctor's office, or somewhere else?

"All will drink from the blood that you provide, Dalia." Kris's voice interrupted my thoughts.

A trail of blood leaked from the vein in my arm as he raised it and led me to the middle of the circle with him. I sensed a shift among the clan as my blood leaked out. I dared not look at them. Kris walked to the first clan member and handed the chalice over. A deep red robe draped over their pale features. Raven-black hair billowed beneath the hood as it fell to her shoulders.

My throat dry as her face was revealed through the shadows. My heart began to beat faster. Why was she here? Vivid's eyes, like two prominent jade stones, glimmered in the moonlight. Her lips covered in my blood turned upwards, and she smiled solemnly. I stared as he passed the chalice to each ominously hooded member, shrouded by the forest's darkness. Was Valentin here? My mind raced with the possibility that he was as each of their hoods fell to their shoulders and they partook of the cup. Vivid, Zayn, Alex, Dayton. Kris stepped in front of the last hooded clan member in the circle. I turned to see all of their eyes were on me.

My jaw clenched as I anticipated who I thought the last member would be. His hood fell onto broad shoulders. I could not forget. The form of his face was branded onto my nightmares. His chin tilted as his maniacal grin was revealed from under the shadows of his hood. My expression may have looked like I had seen death itself. Yet Valentin drank from the cup. His confident demeanor caused my bones to shudder.

His gaze was glued to mine. What did he have planned for tonight? I could see behind his mocking gestures that he was formulating a way of attack. Was this what he was speaking of the night of the concert? Was that encounter just the seed of fear he planted in me for tonight?

Kris walked back to the middle of the circle and held up the chalice to the night sky. Another memory flashed before my eyes as Kris drank from the chalice. My stomach churned at the sight. Was this the same? Was Kris the knight? The one in my dreams, haunting me?

A rush swept through me. Blood smeared on his lips; he threw the chalice to the ground. The same fear that filled me in my dreams rose within my chest. A small blade flicked out from his hand, and he lunged towards me. I jumped back in response to his swift motions. My chest tightened as I stumbled on the brush behind me.

"Now for the living sacrifice." Kris lifted the blade to my neck. My pulse met the slight trickle of blood that escaped. Eyes. Deep dark eyes met mine. Instead of filled with love, they were of hate. Dark eyes. Sweat trickled from his brow as he smiled. A breath into my ear formed the words I could only cause regret to every decision I made up to this point.

"Are you ready to resurrect?"

Death flashed before my eyes as the blade pressed deeper. His hand covered my pulsing vein and lips met mine. I gasped for air as I turned from him. The woman in the painting, a white dress draped her body as the man of darkness hovered over her. My dream of the knight calling me.

"Come away with me." A voice called my name. I am the bride of death. But did I want to be?

My thoughts began to race. Nature proved true as my instinct kicked in despite the excessive blood loss. Adrenaline rushed through me... and I ran. I pulled my heavy legs through the maze of trees before me. I had to get back to the sidewalk. If I was in the public eye again, he couldn't kill me. My chest tightened, and my legs became heavy.

But Kris's booming voice echoed behind me. His words were inaudible yet resounded with fury. I pushed myself to run harder and weaved through the brush. Leaves and dirt crumpled beneath each step. Thorns scratched and pulled every part of me as I stumbled out of the trees and onto the sidewalk.

I plunged into the side of a crowd of drunken partygoers. "Watch out there, young lady," a guy in a pirate costume yelled as I fell by his side.

I didn't care about what he thought. All that mattered was that I was far from Kris and the clan. I was barricaded in by people celebrating Halloween, but like the trees, I weaved my body through the crowded sidewalk. The noise of the streets was ominous, with honking cars, crowds of drunk people, and music booming from each open bar and coffee shop. The noise covered the fact that a young girl was running for her life.

Every movement entrenched around me. I paused for a moment and watched it all. What was the point? Tears trailed down my cheeks as the pain of betrayal hit me. I wasn't running for my life anymore, and my heart let me feel the pain of what just happened. My lungs and entire body were screaming for death. I only wanted true love. But that must not be real. It hurt to know that the one I thought could be my lover for eternity was lying to me. It must be my destiny to die.

I turned my head to take one last glance at the loud, chaotic streets. This wasn't life. It was all so vain. I picked up a steady pace again, even though my lungs screamed for more air. I was determined to ignore how my body ached. I didn't want this life anymore. I thought life with Kris would fulfill me. But it didn't. His love was just a façade. Why did I think there was such a thing as true love, eternal love, anyway?

I heaved open the graveyard gate at Lafayette Cemetery with my last bit of strength. The graveyard rang with the solemn tone of death. Each tombstone I passed was calling me. Their song was to join them. I raced to the gazebo and brushed away some leaves in the farthest corner.

My switchblade was still here. Salvation. I sat on the stone gazebo step. It made sense that this would be the place I would take my final breath. I closed my eyes and imagined what would happen after my last breath. My heart would beat for the last time. I would become hard and lifeless. I would be put six feet under without a care in the world. I'd disappear forever.

My soft skin would become rigid, my lips become blue, and my delicately placed sinews would grow cold. I would lay still until I decayed and disappeared forever. I walked down and out of the gazebo towards the crucifix tombstone. The raven that fell on the tombstone gave me the faith to believe Kris could love me. This is where I would become one with death myself.

My hand caressed the rough cement gazebo wall. I cherished every moment here. Every vampire novel I read, each summer spent reading poetry and walking the gravestones with Elise.

Even the fleeting moments with Kris swirled in my mind. How Kris kissed me and made me his bride. I looked out among the tombstones. Small remembrances of the people that were. The memory, and the decaying bodies inside the ground that I longed to be.

This gazebo could be my final marker. I slumped down next to a nearby tree. Tears still flowed from my face as the cool fall air blew harsh against my cheek. A buzzing from my phone vibrated from my pocket onto my leg. It had to be Elise calling. I pulled my phone out and threw it to the ground. This time, I was serious.

"Don't go," a deep voice sounded behind me. I swallowed hard as I saw no one was around to match the voice. Was I hearing voices now?

"What do you want?" I pulled the blade out from my hand, swiveling around, the knife still sticking out from my arm. "I know you're there. Watch me die! You can't have me!" I shouted into the shadows of the graveyard.

Kris wanted to take me to be his. His promise for me to become his eternal bride pounded through my head, yet betrayal led me to this. I fell to my knees and pulled up my sweater sleeve. The deep red etchings from earlier were still a bright fresh red. The cross on my arm glared back at me. My heart pounded in my chest, and I despised it.

Anger filled me as I looked at the cross. Was it true what the cross meant? To die? It was a lie. All of it was a lie. This cross must be too. "Stop," I heard the voice again.

I placed the blade on my arm and without regret, I cut my wrist. I didn't care. I was truly going to die. I pushed down harder on my arm with the blade, and blood gushed out. Pins and needles tingled through my arm as blood spilled onto the leaves surrounding me. My body jolted. My arm and the ground looked hazed. I blinked. My body fell back, and I felt a pounding in the back of my head as dirt crumbled around my face.

A wave of peace flowed over my body as the prominent rhythm of my heart grew faint. I felt life, my blood, flowing out of my veins. The sky above me glimmered with the faint light left from the stars above until a dark figure hovering over me blocked it. My eyes were heavy as I pulled them open. A final rush swept through my body, as I was alarmed by this figure. I couldn't move myself from it. Or even speak. Stuck in place, I pushed open my eyes only to see that standing above me was the knight.

Chapter
Thirty-Four
The Knight

ETERNITY WAS SUPPOSED TO be forever. That was what I wanted. To be lost in the oblivion of forever. Eternity met me with a pressing warmth, a kiss on my lips. It wasn't as slight as the midnight breeze that caressed my face. The sensation was firm, causing electricity to pulse through my body.

I turned and opened my eyes to blades of grass and shambles of dirt that looked like towers. I felt my chest rise and fall as I breathed in. *I'm not dead?*

Slowly, I lifted myself up from the ground. My body was so light as I moved it upwards like I was floating. I touched my arm and was met with an icy sensation as each finger laid upon it. Every movement I had was airy. My eyes were directed down to see I was in a white chiffon dress. It smoothed around my waist and flowed down to my ankles. As I studied the lace that lightly embroidered my neckline, I touched my chest with the palm of my hand, placing it firmly against my heart.

It felt like a block of ice. I couldn't resist checking, so my hand traveled to the soft part of my neck right below my jawline. I didn't have a pulse. Was I dead? Where was I? I turned my head to look around. Fog blanketed the ground between columns of worn gravestones. Above me was a midnight-blue sky filled with swirling lights. They were like stars but moved along with every gust of wind.

I ran my hand through the grass beneath me. Each blade a vibrant green like I had never seen before. A willow tree's leaves flowed down around me, swaying with each movement of the stars and the subtle wind. Winding branches with the prevalent moonlight seeped in through their cracks.

I studied the light beaming through each branch until one single ray led me to see a single headstone with the words, *"In whom is destined the blackest darkness forever"* etched upon it.

I moved my fingers across the letters, and an amber glow seeped from the words. They lit up as if they were written with fire. What was that? Pulling my hand from the stone, I noticed my fingers were still cold as ice. I had to be dead.

"Come away with me," a voice echoed behind me.

My head turned to find the voice. The knight with his fiery eyes, absent face, and rugged black armor extended his hand toward me. A sense of awe and a force pulled me towards him. I wasn't afraid this time. Every time I saw this knight, I had fear... until now. Did I have to die to lose all fear?

The pulling sensation was something I had never felt before as I walked to the knight and my hand fell into his. The fire in his eyes faded to reveal his face. We both stood in silence as another new sensation came to me. A radiating warmth inside my chest grew. It stopped my breath.

"Who are you?" This question ran through my mind each second. Stuck in awe of him, I couldn't make out the words.

The flesh of his hand was warm against my cold skin. His eyes were so tender and loving. His lips softly formed the phrase again. "Come away with me." They pulled me out of the trance I was in.

"Who are you? Where am I?" I wondered.

With his hand still in mine, he gestured to the ethereal world around me and then to him. He only smiled. "I died for you. You are mine."

The knight exerted power. Goosebumps raised on my arms as he pointed nearby to a black stallion. I could barely make it out compared to what I saw past the fog in the cemetery. Clouds of breath billowed from the stallion's nostrils. The black steed neighed as the knight extended his hand to mine. I reflected back at him with fear as the knight spoke again. "Come, my love. Come away with me."

This time, I would trust. This time, I would let go. This man seemed different than Kris. He was here to help me. The knight led me to the stallion once I nodded at him. He untied the rope confining the stallion to the tree. Deep marbled black hair coated the stallion. His hooves were covered with blackened armor, with a small saddle on his back. The knight bridled the steed quickly.

"Where are we going?" I questioned the knight.

I last remembered being in Lafayette Cemetery, but my memory still felt foggy. I knew that wherever I was, I didn't stand a chance without his guidance. I offered my hand to him in faith that I would be safe. Who knew where I was going? I was probably dead. And if I was, I think where I am going is the right place.

I mounted the horse and clung to the back of the knight as he galloped. His dark metallic armor contrasted against my bare, shivering arms as we approached the darkened forest surrounding us. The knight hit the bridle again, and we sped through the forest.

Weaving through the trees bitterly reminded me of the last moments I had with Kris. Clamoring through the cemetery, running for my life with tears streaming down my face. I tried to feel pain for Kris and for what happened. I closed my eyes and let every memory run through my mind. But I couldn't. I could not feel anything about him. I opened my eyes again with the realization of why I couldn't feel the pain. *I'm dead!*

If only I knew that this entire world was on the other side of death the whole time. I would never have fallen for Kris. Holding onto the knight, his chest kept me sturdy on the back of the stallion. I was dead. I felt no pain. Joy flooded me as my thoughts reeled. This was the same knight from my dreams. He was calling me all along. It was him. He never wanted me to feel pain, or regret, only love. That's why he was calling me!

I let my arms clasps harder around his waist as he slowed the steed down through a clearing. The darkness of the forest waned to reveal a desolate field. It was lifeless, barren, and grey. We slowly rode onwards to a castle in the middle of the field. The beams of the castle loomed over us. Grey cobblestone bricks cast an ominous presence as a chain-bridge lowered. I had never been so close to such a towering building. I grabbed the knight's hand tightly for reassurance. He pulled me down from the steed and motioned for me to follow him.

"This is where I am taking you. You must wait for me here... before our wedding day."

Wedding day? I stumbled and couldn't make out any words to say. Despite my hesitations put upon me by the dredging look of the castle and the prospect of marriage, I still followed him across the bridge and through a large wooden door. It was all too fast for me to see everything, but I felt like I had seen this all before. The knight led me up winding brick steps to a single bedroom. My heart began to pound fast. This was familiar to me. Finally, the knight opened the door to a room, and I gasped. This was the room from my dreams. The mirror, the scarlet-red dress draped across a wooden chair, and the window overlooking the field.

I walked over to the window to gaze out. But the knight stopped me as he held my hand. "This is for you." He held a golden chain with a pendant across my chest. I looked in the mirror. Reflected back at me were the same green eyes and pale complexion framed by black hair. Dying didn't change my appearance much. I looked down at the chain the knight held across my chest.

A single ruby-red pendant adorned my neck. A sense of electricity began at my chest with the pendant and swept through my entire body.

The knight leaned in close and whispered into my ear, "My blood for you."

Chapter Thirty-Five

Immortal

A POUNDING IN MY head grew. Blood rushed through my veins, oxygen replenished my lungs, and my arms filled with warmth. The pounding was my heart. I shook under the waves of my body being pulled into life. The heartbeat resounding in my head got louder with each passing second. I clenched my fists together to resist it. I wanted nothing but to die. I wanted nothing more than to stop what was happening in my body. I didn't want this life. Why did this have to happen to me?

I opened my eyes to a cloud-filled sky. No majestic lights swirling above. Willow tree leaves swaying with the wind had disappeared. Dead leaves crunched off my sweater and fell down to the dirt beneath me. No vibrant-colored hues of the earth or grass anymore. And... wait... ouch! My head was pounding with the worst migraine in all history!

I could feel pain! Why was I here? Was it just a dream with the knight, or did I really die and come back? But how could I? Why did I? My body ached to the bone. I tugged my dusty black sleeve up on my right arm. My wrist was smooth with no cut marks at all. No wounds. All that was left were the remnants of blood smeared across my skin. Dried blood sloughing off smooth skin.

My jaw dropped, and I rushed to pull up my other sleeve. Nothing at all. Was I doomed to live forever? How could I NOT DIE? I wanted to go back! I already missed the pure feeling of love I had from being there. Now I was left to feel pain. I wanted to go back! I pounded my wrist against a tombstone next to me and leaned into it bitterly.

My phone buzzing in my pocket caused me to jump. Taking a deep breath, I pulled it out. I was relieved as I looked down at the text. Elise had called about nine times. Her single text displayed across the screen. *"Are you OK? Can you answer my calls?"*

I could practically hear her frantic voice as I read it. My call before passing out must have caused her to worry. Hell, she *should* be worried. What was I doing? Still disgusted, and not ready to explain myself to Elise, I tucked my phone back in my pocket. She wouldn't want to know I was here or that I tried to commit suicide. The only thing she would be happy about was that I failed at it again.

I dragged myself up from the ground. My head pounded, and my vision slowly caught up with me as I stood. I used the stone gazebo railing to stabilize myself as my weak knees settled in. The inside of the gazebo was dark and empty. It usually was until last night. I reeled through every moment with Kris in my mind. The darkened gazebo now became a marker of my pain of betrayal. Wait, maybe...?

I lifted my black ribbon choker that I wore solely for the purpose of covering my initiation wound. Only the smooth skin of my neck met my fingers. The initiation wound from last night with Kris had disappeared too?!

I paced back a couple of steps, and my hand raised to my forehead to catch myself from falling forward. I swallowed hard, allowing every second I breathed and thought to sink in. All the cuts from the initiation, the sacrifice, and even my own attempts at death had somehow disappeared. How could this be? How could I not die? Unless what happened to me was what Kris talked about.

I gave myself over to the clan and made a vow for eternal life. Then I died, and I resurrected. This has to be exactly like Kris said would happen if I died. Did I resurrect as a vampire? My breath became heavy, and I staggered back a step, almost collapsing again. Now... I couldn't die. If this was real, and I was a vampire, then I could never die!

I turned to the ground and kicked the hardened earth beneath me. I ached for the peace I felt in death. I could never return to the amazing place with the knight. My eyes began to swell with tears. Why was life so bitter to me? Why did death always escape me? I placed my hand on my chest. It was still there. No matter how I tried, this detestable heart kept beating. What would I do as a vampire now that the clan had turned on me? There was no way I could go back. I might as well be dead.

I looked up at the cloud-filled sky again. Wait! It was still... dark out? How much time had really passed while I was dead? Kris said it would take three days before I would resurrect into a vampire. I pulled my phone from my pocket. Green lights illuminated the words that caught me off guard.

'October 31st... 8:22 p.m.' I've been here for maybe an hour?

I stared hard down at my wrists, amazed that there was nothing but clean skin. Not even an inkling that I had cut. Did the knight do this? Was I alive because of him? I touched my chest again. The red pendant! The last words he spoke to me rang through my spirit. He was the one who brought me back to life, through the red pendant. But what did it mean? What was a red pendant for?

212

I wasn't sure what or who this knight that had been perpetuating my dreams was. I placed my hand on my throbbing head again. A slight lightning bolt in the distance caused me to jump. Crap! The unpredictable weather here in New Orleans. I raced to the cemetery's tall winding gate and peeped out to see the sidewalk. No Kris... or Valentin. At least it was dark enough outside, and I could easily mask myself in between the lights and crowds.

I caught sight of the cathedral down the street between the drizzling rain. Shelter! There was no way Kris would go into a church! Truthfully, I detested churches. I couldn't ever bring myself to a place as pious as a cathedral, except for tonight. Running away from Kris, or the clan, was the last thing I ever thought I would be doing tonight.

The pain of it all hit me as I dragged my heavy boots across the pavement. I trusted Kris. Not only that, I loved Kris. Yet he betrayed me. The slight drizzle of rain soon became a heavy downpour. I ran faster, pushing myself between the crowds of people seeking an escape from the rain as well. I tried my best to be shrouded by darkness and kept my face down with each streetlight I passed. I finally reached the cathedral's towering door.

A sharp pain filled my chest as I struggled to breathe after running. Exactly. Someone as vile as myself couldn't even be near a church without having a heart attack! I held my hands over my chest, breathed in deeply, and waited for the pain to disappear. The towering cathedral doors were perfectly symmetrical to the rest of the building. The torrenting rain soaking my clothes urged me to open them. Still, I couldn't make myself open them yet.

Why did Kris do this to me? Why was I here alone on Halloween night? Was there any way this could be mended? Tears began to well from my eyes and were washed away by the rain. I brushed them away with the hair plastered to the side of my face. I needed to at least get out of this rain. Every inch of my clothes, hair, and skin were soaked. I rationalized to myself and pulled the large bronze door handle.

Of course, it was locked. Pain in my chest hit me again. This time, as the pain twinged in my body, a voice behind me spoke in unison with it.

"Life is within the blood..."

Kris? My breath shortened, as I twisted the doorknob harder. The door wouldn't budge under my weak, wet hands. My heart began beating faster, and I turned to face him. Only the haze of heavy raindrops was behind me. There was nothing there. I pushed on the cathedral door with all my strength and twisted the handle hard. A clicking noise came as the handle gave way and I plummeted inside. I turned the lock on the door just in case.

Glimpsing behind me again, I saw no one. Now, I was seriously going crazy. I could swear I heard a voice behind me. The small corridor inside had candles lining each side of the entrance. A second doorway was before me. A faint echoing of voices in the distance stopped me. My breath suddenly became heavy. *He's here!* I hurriedly yanked the door back, placing my cold hand on my forehead. Kris was playing games with me. I needed to get away before he found me. Every noise I made suddenly became more noticeable. The door hinges creaking, the breath leaving my nose, even the rain dripping from my jacket onto the floor sounded like tidal waves. Panic began to set in as I leaned against the door. I couldn't let this happen!

Holding my back to the wooden door frame, I dared not move an inch until I could think of what to do. I looked at the shadows of the candle flames dancing across the corridor walls. Then it hit me: This place looked just like my dream. The corridor the knight led me through was here. I shut my eyes as peace ran through me. Could this just be the answer I was looking for?

I turned and placed my shaking hand on the metal doorknob. The clan could be in there, encircling every corner of the room, ready to pounce on me. I shut my eyes again. Or there was the chance that the knight was real. He would be standing in the chapel, waiting to save me from this world. What did I have to lose? I pushed my weight against the large wooden door, and a sharp pain hit my chest again.

The metal hinges echoed through the cathedral as I pushed open the door. Dark pillars symmetrically placed on each column lined the walls. A large window let in the moonlight to shine perfectly on a large crucifix at the altar. Empty wooden pews, shrines to old men, and a crucifix. No knight, no clan, no Kris. Just an empty cathedral. I exhaled slowly in relief.

I stepped in and let the door close behind me. There was nothing to fear. I must be hearing things because of the amount of stress I've been under. There was no other explanation. I would have never imagined myself here, even last night. Tears streamed down my face as I remembered the vow I made. The blood I gave to Kris was my life for him. His blood given to me was his life.

I wanted to love him... but I couldn't. It only brought a stake through my broken heart. A scratching noise caught me off guard. I turned to look at the empty room surrounding me. What was that? The light from the window dimmed, and darkness covered the room. I wasn't alone. My body stiffened as I closed my eyes.

"Life is within the blood," a voice whispered behind me.

Chapter Thirty-Six
Eternity

My breath escaped me. The words sliced me into pieces. Every word I spoke in commitment to him. *You can have my life, my blood. It's yo*urs. Last night's events played through my mind like a horror flick, haunting me. I couldn't go back on my vow with Kris. There was no way I could escape this.

"Life is within the blood." The voice so strong I opened my eyes and turned to make sure no one was here. There was nothing. No one. Only the large crucifix hanging before me. Was what Kris said about the living sacrifice true? Did the cross have any meaning? I walked down the aisle, between the pews and up to the altar. There had to be some reason I was here. A living sacrifice was giving one's blood and giving your life for another. Kris had given up all his body and soul to the clan. My eyes scanned every inch of the large cross. Was this a living sacrifice too?

Voices echoing behind the door pulled me from my thoughts. This time, I couldn't make out what it was saying.

"Who's there?" I responded to the voice this time, trying to keep my words steady.

I scanned my eyes across the back of the sanctuary. Shadows in every corner of the room could conceal anyone hiding in them. I waited as no one reacted to my question. What if the clan was here to get me? A lightning bolt struck the window above the crucifix, causing a tingling sensation to run over every inch of my body. Pain darted through my chest. The distant voices echoed again with a whisper this time. It was so soft and slid across my ears.

"Life is within the blood." The phrase rang within my spirit. A heaviness filled my chest with the pain that still lingered. God... what is happening to me? My knees hit the hard brick-laden floor and looked up at the Jesus figure on the cross. The living sacrifice began reeling through my mind again. The memories closed in on me like a coffin. I had made a covenant of darkness with the clan. Was there any hope? Was this what loving Kris led me to? A darkness inside that I could no longer contain?

No! I pounded my fist into the ground. My only hope was in the one I saw after death. I gasped for another breath, struggling to look up at the cross again. The sharp pain in my chest stopped as the darkness expelled from within me. My vision faded, and my body began to shake under the heaviness. What was happening to me? I touched my eyelids; am I a vampire? I could only see darkness before me. In the shadows, a man appeared. He was stripped, his skin cut open, revealing pieces of bones and organs. Blood shimmered with crimson as lighting bolted around him. A stream of blood flowed from his side.

His arms painfully stretched out as nails protruded from each hand. "My blood for you." The words were spoken close to my ear this time. His eyes were hollow and grieved as he looked down at me. They pierced my soul as they turned into flames of fire. My body jolted.

"The eyes of fire. The knight!" I spread my arms open as the man on the cross did. My hands shook as I stretched them out and a sweet peace filled me. "You can have my life, my blood. It's yours."

A harrowing noise left my lungs and reverberated within every fiber of my being. A scream escaped my mouth as pure joy swept through me. I could only see the faded cross on the desolate altar. It was him! He was the one who gave himself up for me. He was the living sacrifice! I didn't have to give my blood to him. He was the one who gave his blood to me!

Rays of light danced across my face as they shone from behind the crucifix. The light pierced me just as the light penetrated my emotions. An echo of a voice in the corridor caught me off guard.

A voice I recognized. "Dalia?" I turned to see Elise running toward me. My body felt stiff, frozen. I couldn't leave this place.

Christ was the knight in my dreams. What he offered on the cross was his life blood for me. His blood, his love was for me. He was the living sacrifice. He loved me. His very life was given in his blood for me. For eternity.

Epilogue

BLOOD DRIPPED FROM MY hands and feet onto the cemetery grass. My sweat turned to blood with the prayer that turned my soul to pieces. My love for *her* brought me here to a cemetery covered in worn gravestones.

Soft grass glistened from earlier dew that reflected the moonlight. Below the dew a simple reflection of the bodies entrapped below. Just like the swirling stars above burned, each soul below burned. If only they could rise and shine with fire as the stars do. If only they knew it was the flame of my love.

I ran through the crumbled and worn gravestones, ignoring the pain that the sacrifice had on my body. I came here to know the darkness that entangled her when I became the sacrifice. But death couldn't conquer me. Nothing was too hard for my bride, and I picked up my pace a little more. I passed grave after countless grave. I was seeking only one tonight. The immense pain that I went through to get here was worth it. *She* was worth it.

A hollow wind crossed my face and startled the leaves surrounding a tree. Before me, a willow tree's leaves swayed around a single gravestone. My heart struck within me as I could only remember it as the grave of my bride. The darkness entangled her and swallowed her up in the grip of death itself. Scrawled upon the gravestone were the very words that chained her. *"In whom is destined the blackest darkness forever."*

My whole being enraged at this thought. The law of sin and death condemned her to this grave. The sentence that brought eternal separation. Time was my only enemy, as I waited for this moment for what felt to be an eternity. I would not let her go. I bent on one knee and gazed into the consequence of this fallen world. A tattered dress covered her body, her hollowed eyes cold and dark. The flames of hell illuminated the graves around us as I slid my hand across her worn cheek. A streak of my blood painted across her face. Her chest raised as the blood marked her skin. Just one drop of my blood, the very life of God, came and filled her lungs for the first time in ages. The curse of death could not counter my blood.

My lips burned to touch hers again. I turned her face towards me, with the knowledge that on the inside she was screaming from the depths for me to reawaken her again. My eyes filled with passion as I breathed in the humid cemetery air. My devotion for her filled my veins. It was the very blood that spilled from my hands. I positioned my face close to hers. Breath exuded from my lungs and filled her own. My flaming eyes began to burn and open hers. Blood fell from the crown upon my head, it covered hers. With all the strength within my bones left, my lips finally met hers.

Our kiss was met with a jolt of pure power as love surged from my being. Righteousness beheld her countenance, as her jade-green eyes opened. Her spirit reawakened from the curse of death at last. The tattered shreds covering her bare body transformed into a beautiful white robe. The stitches and sinews of thread clothed her resurrected body. Not even a smudge of darkness remained within her. Her worn face now held a calm demeanor.

I stretched out my hand to her. "Come away with me."

Her eyes trailed over the burning tombstones and the souls screaming from within them. I turned her chin towards me.

"Look into my eyes, my bride. This is the fire that will carry you through. My fire will carry you to eternity." My words calmed her wandering gaze. All her trust must be put into me.

She looked back and forth at the death and destruction surrounding her as she had been awakened to the world around her. With my blood upon her head, the pangs of death threatened her no more. She held a candid smile as the touch of my hand, my guidance, filled her with peace.

I whispered into her ear, "Follow me."

I touched her lips once more. My presence filled her with hope in the midst of the ashes as I guided her through the graves and to my black stallion tied to the tree. We mounted the stallion. My bride clenched onto my back, her warm hands clasped tightly to my tattered gray tunic, holding on for the life within her. I knew her every prayer was just to stay with me, to be with me, to seek me. A cold chill from the wind ran through me as I faced the darkened forest surrounding us.

Light emanating before us kept us going as we darted through trees and heavy brush. My eyes turned to flames as they did when I first saw my bride. We were close to the end of the forest and to the kingdom that awaited her. The hooves from my steed hit the rough forest ground, as the darkness of the trees slowly began to fade. A wave of the presence of life diminished every inch of darkness. The light from before us removed it all. Here it is. Our time has come. Our kingdom before us. My death, my sacrifice of love became her ultimate victory.

Acknowledgements

It took only 6 months for Eternal Love to be written. Getting it ready and edited for publication took much longer. Many people contributed to the making of Eternal Love

The Eternal Love family is listed below :

My parents, you helped me become an avid reader/writer. I am grateful for the start you gave me.

Brian Welch, your story was a saving grace for me. Thank you for your bravery and for sharing your testimony. Rock on!

Ellen Schreiber, my all-time favorite author. You made me into a book nerd and have inspired me so much.

Robert Smith and The Cure, your music inspired so many chapters of this book.

Lisa Saunders- my mother-in-love who helped edit, market, and ultimately believed in me so much.

Emma Greene – the first of many living dead girls. A daughter of God, She believed in my book and helped me finish.

Victoria Jane, wonderful Developmental Editor at victoriajaneeditorial.com

Ashley Olivier copy line editor at Enchanted Author Services. http://www.ashleyoliviereditor.com

Book Cover Art created by Artscandcare

Cameron Fox with Foxc Photography, for the amazing author picture.https://foxc.photography/

My beloved friend Audrey Dutton, my sister in Christ, for all the amazing adventures we had. Especially the one that inspired this book.

My friend Rachel, for her wonderful friendship. You are my Elise.

My friend Betsy, a precious daughter of God, and a hippie at heart. Thank you for your insight, editing, and guiding words.

My sweet husband Nivik, who loves me eternally.

About the author

Danielle Wolfe's love for books began in her teenage years, igniting a lifelong dream to write her own paranormal romance. Blending her fascination with vampires along with her faith, she creates stories that bring hope to those who are suffering. Now, as a homeschooling mother of two, she continues to pursue her dreams with the support of her husband, Nivik. Her debut novel, Eternal Love, emerged from a deeply personal journey of finding light in the midst of her own darkness.

You can find out more about Danielle's upcoming books at https://daniellewolfebooks.com/

If you enjoyed reading this book or even if you didn't, please leave a review! It will help my book get into the hands of more readers!

Review on Goodreads or on Amazon, please!

www.ingramcontent.com/pod-product-compliance
Lightning Source LLC
Chambersburg PA
CBHW010827250626
47169CB00010B/2987

* 9 798991 650021 *